EDEN'S WARRIORS

LLOYD TACKITT

Eden's Warriors
Copyright © 2013 by Lloyd Tackitt. All rights reserved.
First Kindle Edition: April 2013

Cover and Formatting: Streetlight Graphics

This is a work of fiction. Names, characters, places, and incidents either are the product of the author's imagination or are used fictitiously, and any resemblance to locales, events, business establishments, or actual persons—living or dead—is entirely coincidental.

CHAPTER 1

LINING UP THE FRONT SIGHT just below the kidnapper's chin, he knew that at this short distance the bullet would enter slightly above the man's eyebrows, centered between them. He gently squeezed off the first shot, not waiting to see if the bullet hit its target or not; he knew it did, he didn't miss at this range. Instead of watching the first man go down, Adrian swung his rifle slightly to the left and shot the second man in the chest, no time for pin-point aiming now that the action had started.

The third kidnapper dove behind a downed tree. The tree was too small; Adrian had a good view of the man's back and shot him in the near-side shoulder blade, the bullet exiting at an angle that took out heart and lung.

The three shots rolled out like one long extended shot, the third echoing through the forest and into silence.

For a long, long moment, nothing stirred. No birds flew or sang, no squirrel scampered up a tree. Every living creature had frozen in place. Then the older of the two girls stood up, holding up her hands, showing they were tied, having the clarity of mind to try to keep from being shot by someone that might be overly excited.

She needn't have worried. Adrian wasn't excited. He had merely executed an action that needed to be performed. He watched from cover for another thirty seconds, waiting to see if anything else needed to be done.

The second girl stood. She was much younger, maybe seven or eight. The older girl looked to be in her early teens, maybe fourteen. They weren't trail dirty, their hands and faces were clean. Their clothes weren't new, but weren't torn or soiled. Adrian noted that the two girls' facial expressions were those of scared girls, not of victims. *They couldn't have been captured more than a few hours ago.* He thought to himself.

Adrian signaled Bear, his wolf, to move ahead. Bear would let him know if there was anyone else about.

Moving slowly from cover, Adrian allowed the girls to see him for the first time. He kept his rifle at the ready position just in case, but smiled as largely as he could as he approached.

"What's wrong with your face?" asked the older girl. "Stop that, you're scaring my sister!"

Adrian stopped smiling. He was relieved to do so; it didn't feel any more natural than it apparently looked. He said "Sorry, I was trying to smile, so you would know I wasn't going to hurt you."

The younger girl said "If that was a smile, it was the scariest one I ever saw."

At this Adrian grinned, a genuine expression of amusement. The older girl said "Now that's tons better, mister." The little girl nodded and grinned back at Adrian.

"Ok, where's your family? I want to get you home before dark, if possible."

"No family." the youngest one said. "Our family died long time ago."

The older girl spoke up. "Our parents died three years ago, both of them. We've been making out pretty well on our own since. Until these assholes showed up." The way she used the word asshole so naturally made Adrian raise an eyebrow.

The girl continued. "They snuck up on us while we were asleep. They must have watched us for a while first. That was early this morning. They wanted to get away from our homestead in case any family or friends showed up. I think they were getting ready to rape us when you shot them."

Adrian paused for a long while before speaking again. He thought the best thing would be to take them back to their home, check around for any reliable adults that would keep an eye on them. "My name is Adrian." He said. "What's yours?"

"Adrian?" the older girl asked. "You wouldn't be Adrian Hunter, would you? You look like the description we've heard of General Bear, what with that scar on your cheek, and that pet wolf."

Adrian, surprised at being recognized by two girls in the middle of nowhere, said "Yeah, Adrian Hunter. How in the world did you..."

"You're famous. Everyone knows about you, they talk about you all the time. How you defeated all those cannibals in Colorado by yourself with just a sharp stick, and killed all those raiders from Louisiana, hundreds of them. Mostly they talk about you sleeping with grizzly bears and having cubs by them. They don't say that right in front of us, of course, but we hear them when they think we don't."

"How could those stories travel like that?" Adrian wondered aloud.

"Ham radio operators." The younger girl answered as though he was asking her. "There are a lot of ham radios, and there isn't much for them to talk about on them except stories of what's happening in their areas. Most of that stuff is dull as ditchwater. Had some rain, need some rain, wish it would rain...stuff like that. When a really good story comes along, it gets talked about a lot. You've been making some really good stories for folks to talk about."

"I might as well have a tattoo on my forehead," Adrian said, shaking his head. "Well ladies, how about I escort you back home? Do you know the way back?" Then bowing in a mock courtly manner he said, "Oh and by the way, you seem to need no introduction from me, but you have me at a disadvantage. May I ask your names?"

"Lila." stated the older one, "and this is Rita. Sure we know the way back, follow us."

"Wait up a second." Adrian said. "Let's get whatever is useful from the bodies and camp."

It didn't take long to gather the kidnappers' weapons and food. The weapons were of poor quality and in poor condition, but would still be useful to someone. Rifles and ammunition were the best items to trade for food, and these would be useful for at least that much. The kidnappers' food supply was mostly home-canned vegetables. No meat. Vegetables were good for the nutrients they held, but poor on calories. *Better than nothing, but not by much.* Adrian thought to himself.

Without a backward glance at the three bodies, the two girls climbed onto Adrian's horse. He took the reins and started walking east. *These are tough kids; they don't seem fazed by being kidnapped or the sudden violence of three men dying ugly deaths right at their feet. It's a cinch they've not led easy lives.*

After several hours and just before dark Adrian called a halt. "Let's camp here ladies. Are you hungry? I have food."

Rita said "Yes, please. We ate supper last night, but they got us before we woke up, so no breakfast or lunch. I would really like a drink of water, if that's okay?"

This little girl talks like an adult, she must be extraordinarily intelligent. In fact both of them seem to be. Adrian passed his canteen, then dug into his backpack and removed a cloth-wrapped package that contained a bag of deer pemmican that his Aunt Sarah had given him for the road; he'd been on the road for nearly three weeks, so there wasn't much left in the bag. He also had some of the battle rations that had been made up for the fight with Rex's Louisiana raiders, but while they were nutritious, they didn't taste at all good. Adrian thought the girls would like the pemmican better; it was fairly tasty, besides being loaded with calories.

"You girls set up camp, gather wood and start a fire," said Adrian. "There should be a creek at the bottom of this slope. I'll water the horse and be back in a little bit. We should get to your house sometime tomorrow morning."

Lila and Rita nodded their understanding; their mouths too full of pemmican to speak.

After he returned from watering the horse, Adrian stoked the fire, then spread his bedroll out for the girls to share. It was the middle of spring and the nights were cool but not cold; Adrian would nap off-and-on during the night leaning against a tree.

He watched as the girls finished eating and there was nothing left to do but go to sleep or sit and stare into the fire and talk.

Either they are exceptionally cool, or they put on a great act. If it's an act it will probably break down around bed time. Once they stop moving, the reality will sink in extra hard.

The little one fell asleep almost immediately. Lila stayed awake, sitting up and holding Rita's small hand. She looked up from the fire at Adrian and said softly, "We really don't have much to go back to. We planted the garden and put in a crop of corn, but grasshoppers have pretty much done it in. We've about used up our root cellar supplies, and those assholes destroyed what they couldn't carry, and they couldn't carry enough to amount to nothing."

Adrian asked just as softy, not wanting to wake Rita, "Do you have any relatives or friends that'll take you in?"

"No relatives at all. Friends? Sure, some. But not any that can afford two more mouths to feed. I think some of them might try, but we'd just drag them down. That's why we were living on our own. Thought we could make out and not drag some poor family down trying to help us. We came close to making it. Hadn't of been for the grasshoppers and the assholes we would have scratched by somehow, this year anyway."

Adrian thought for a long time before speaking. Lila seemed to have decided Adrian wasn't going to talk any more that night because she jumped a little when he did. "It's quite a dilemma," he said. "I can't take you with me, and I can't leave you behind. I'm on a trip to nowhere in particular, other than a stop in Corpus Christi to look around."

"Are you going to marry Linda when you get back?"

Surprised, Adrian asked, "How do you know about Linda?"

"Everything you do gets talked about on the ham radios and then spreads. You and Linda are one of the best stories about you, and everyone is talking about it. It's like a soap opera, only real"

"Well sh...crap. This has gotten ridiculous. Everyone knows my business better than I do. Look, I can feed you two, but who knows what dangers lay ahead? Trouble seems to find me at regular intervals; going with me could get you badly hurt or dead. But staying behind...doesn't sound promising either. We'll take a look at your house tomorrow, maybe visit some of your neighbors. Hopefully something will work clear by then. You go on to sleep now, tomorrow could be a hard day." *Could be a difficult day for all of us.*

Adrian woke the girls the next morning when he built the fire up and put tea on to boil. Using a small camper's coffee pot he boiled water, then carefully measured in tea leaves that his uncle Roman had grown and cured. He missed coffee, figured he would probably miss it the rest of his life, but the strong, bitter tea was almost as good.

The girls shared the tea with him. Passing the

cup back and forth, taking small sips of the strong hot brew. He was out of pemmican—the girls had eaten all that was left—and was down to the battle rations. Adrian offered a piece of a ration bar to each girl, explaining as he offered, "This doesn't taste good, but it has a lot of calories. It's good fuel, if not good food."

He grinned at Rita's expression as she bit into the bar. Lila, seeing Rita's frown, was better prepared and tried to hide her disgusted expression as she took a bite. Other than a tightening around her eyes, she did a good job of keeping her face deadpan.

When they arrived at the girls' home a few hours later, Adrian knew he wouldn't be leaving them there. The ramshackle, rundown mobile home wasn't worth trying to repair. It had never been a very good place in its best days, and after three years of the girls trying to make it on their own, it was a disaster. The meager garden had been decimated by insects. What few leaves were left looked like lacework. The corn crop, a small field of maybe half an acre, was drought-stunted, and had been finished off by grasshoppers, just as they'd said. There was no chance of a crop.

Adrian checked out the root cellar. The kidnappers had destroyed everything they didn't take, but there couldn't have been much anyway. Even if it had been full, and the contents undamaged, the girls would have been out of food in three or four weeks. One way or another, their time on this homestead had been coming to a quick end.

Emerging from the root cellar, he asked Lila "Where's the nearest family you think might take you in?"

She pointed to the south and said "Zachary's, about an hour and a half."

Adrian said, "Lead the way." *Lord, I hope these Zachary's are good people.*

CHAPTER 2

ADRIAN LED THE HORSE CARRYING the two girls to the edge of the trees. From there it was open ground to Zachary's cabin. He walked into the open a few yards before stopping and calling out.

"Hello the house! Anyone home?" Then he waited, and watched the smoke drifting lazily from the cabin's chimney. *They're home alright, and suspicious of strangers. As they should be.*

Adrian shouted again, and stood waiting. After another minute, a tall, thin man dressed in overalls and a tee-shirt, stepped out from behind the cabin. He was holding a lever-action rifle pointed towards Adrian. The rifle was in an extremely ready position, not quite shouldered, but not far from it, either. The man yelled back at Adrian "Come on in, but slowly, and keep your hands where I can see them."

Adrian began moving again, slowly as he'd been told, keeping his left hand at shoulder height, holding the reins out in front of him with his right hand. When he'd closed the distance to only fifty feet between him and the man, the man said, in voice filled with suspicion, "Lila, is that you and Rita? What you girls doing with this here man, eh?"

"It's alright Mr. Zachary, he helped us when we was kidnapped yesterday." Lila replied.

"Kidnapped? Who took you girls? Who is this man? I don't recognize him." Mr. Zachary asked.

"Why this here is General Bear, all the way from the Colorado cannibal fight and just recently from killing those Louisiana raiders!" shouted Rita with obvious pleasure.

"General Bear?" Mr. Zachary asked. "Really?"

Adrian groaned inwardly, but answered. "Yes sir, I'm Adrian Hunter. I'm on my way to Corpus Christi, and came across these ladies yesterday in a bit of a situation. From the looks of their home they'd only starve if I left them there. I'm hoping to find someone to take them in; they said you're the nearest decent neighbor, so I brought them to you."

By this time, Mr. Zachary had closed the distance between them and was sticking his hand out for Adrian to shake, his rifle almost forgotten in the crook of his arm. "By golly, this is something. Wait 'till Ma sees who stopped by, she'll be tickled pink— and you best be hungry, cause she's going to feed you whether you like it or not."

Rita said, "We'll like it Mr. Zachary, we'll like it a lot! Mrs. Zachary is a fine cook!"

"Well come on in the house and let me introduce you to my family. They'll all be plumb thrilled at this." Mr. Zachary turned and walked swiftly towards the cabin shouting "Ma! Guess who's here!"

Adrian sopped up the last of the black-eyed pea juice with a corn dodger and happily ate it. He leaned back and said "Mrs. Zachary that was extremely good. Best eating I've had in weeks. Little Rita was dead right, you are a fine cook."

Blushing with pleasure, Mrs. Zachary replied, "Well it wasn't much really, but I'm proud you enjoyed it. We don't get many visitors, and never seen one as famous as you. I'll have bragging rights for years to come. Sure you don't want some buttermilk pie?"

Adrian groaned. "I want some, yes ma'am, but there's no room for it yet. Maybe I could take you up on that later?"

Adrian had learned that Mr. Zachary's name was Roger, but Mrs. Zachary had been introduced as Ma, and that seemed to be the only name she went by. The three Zachary boys and the father all called her that. He had also quickly discovered that she ran the family—she would be the one to decide whether they took in the girls or not.

"Ma" Adrian said, "We need to do a bit of talking if you don't mind."

Lila spoke up "Rita, let's go outside and play. The grownups want to talk without us listening."

Ma added, "You boys go outside too, scat now!"

After the five children had left the table and gone outside, Ma said, "I know what you're going to ask, and much as I hate it, the answer is no. I can't take those girls in, and it's not just food either. Take a look out that window. You see how my oldest boy is mooning over that girl? Hormones are flying fast and furious right now. Those young'uns are cauldrons of bubbling hormones at that age. Putting those girls under the same roof with these boys would be a natural disaster. They didn't grow up together; they don't have that natural aversion to each other they'd have if they had. No sir, I'm sorry as I can be to say no to you on this...but it can't be."

Adrian, looking out the window, could clearly see what Ma was saying was true. The oldest boy and Lila were obviously interested in each other, more than the two kids understood. Adrian opened his mouth to ask a question, but before he could utter a sound, Ma interrupted.

"There isn't a family anywhere near here that I know of that could take them in. Either they can't feed them, or they aren't good people, or they have the same problem I have, boys of a certain age. I don't know of a family I could send you to and have any hope of them taking the girls in, or that I would want to take those nice girls in. Not one." She paused, then continued thoughtfully. "I've heard about a girl's orphanage two or three days travel from here. I don't know nothing about it, but it's been mentioned a time or two by travelers. If you're going to Corpus Christi it's more or less on your way, isn't it Pa?"

Roger said, "I'd guess three days south of here from what I've heard. That'll take you off your southeast course some, but I don't think you'd lose more than a day. Just head south from here and stop occasionally to ask where it's at, and I expect you'll find it easy enough."

It took four days, Adrian walking while the girls rode the horse and Bear roamed around them as usual, for them to find their way to the orphanage. It was a large two story house, reminiscent of a smaller plantation mansion more than a normal residence. *Probably has dozens of rooms for the girls.* A woman in her late fifties opened to his knock. She wore a full length dress and reminded Adrian of a typical grandmother. "Yes?" She asked. "Can I help you?"

Adrian replied. "Yes ma'am, I sure hope so. I found these two girls in trouble about a week ago, and I'm looking for a good home for them. I hear that this is a girl's orphanage? Is that true?"

Smiling brightly, the woman stuck her hand out to shake and said, "I'm Lacy, Lacy Calhoun. You and your girls come on inside and sit while we talk."

The living room was large, dark, and formal. It had a coolness to it that spoke of never seeing sunlight, and indeed, the few windows were heavily curtained. Even though it was nearly noon, Lacy lit two lamps for light to talk by.

Lacy said, "We don't call this place an orphanage, we call it a 'home for young ladies.' There have been so many of them that have been stranded from family and loved ones by these hard times. We—that's my brother, Reggie, and myself—take in some girls, but they have to be healthy and able-bodied because they have to work quite hard in the fields to raise the food they eat. We have fourteen young ladies with us now, from ten to eighteen years old. They're out in the vegetable patch with Reggie now, but they'll all be coming in soon for lunch. You can join us if you'd like, and meet everyone."

She looked directly at Adrian, her hands folded quietly on her lap, and continued.

"As to what I am sure is on your mind right now, yes I do have room for these two lovely girls, as long as they are as healthy as they look. It may seem cold, but we get by on what we can do for ourselves.

Taking in someone who is sick or weak endangers all of us. But these girls look fine."

When the girls came in Lacy introduced first Lila and Rita and then Adrian. She made a big deal out of Adrian being General Hunter. The girls all looked at him with a renewed interest. When almost everyone was seated at the large dining table, two of the older girls began serving the simple meal, consisting of stew with very little meat but lots of vegetables, and cornbread on the side.

Adrian looked the brother over thoroughly. He was a tall, thin, man, slightly older than his sister. He was informal and comfortable with the girls at the table. But his hands, Adrian noticed, weren't calloused from work, and that began a buzzing in the back of his mind that something might not be completely right about this situation. With that forewarning he began to observe everything more carefully. His eagerness to rid himself of the responsibility of two young girls had, to this point, clouded his attentiveness to detail. Now, however, he was alert again.

He watched the resident girl's faces closely without being obvious about it. As Lacy announced to the girls that they would be taking in these two new girls, Adrian saw traces of sorrow on more than one of their faces. The most interesting was the oldest girl, who was sitting in a position where neither Lacy or Reggie were watching her. She made a strange face at Adrian, widening and then moving here eyes from side to side as though to tell him something—certainly something she couldn't say in front of either Lacy or Reggie.

Adrian couldn't signal back without giving her away; instead he said "I'll be getting on the road right after we eat. I can't tell you how much I appreciate your kindness and generosity in taking in Lila and Rita. I'm sure they'll be fine here." He saw the oldest girl's face fall as she obviously thought that either he didn't understand her warning or didn't care.

Adrian gave the two girls each a quick hug and kiss on the cheek. Rita shed a few tears and said in a trembling voice, "Will you come see us sometime?"

Adrian wanted to say yes, but Lacy was listening with extra intensity for Adrian's answer and he didn't want her to think he would be back this way.

"No little Rita, I don't expect to be coming this way again. But when you get all grown up you can come visit me at Fort Brazos." It was a hard thing to leave the girls thinking he wouldn't be back. He would stick around a while, watching from out of sight, to see what was going on in this place. Maybe the oldest girl was warning him of something bad, or maybe she wasn't right in the head. He'd wait and watch, and see for himself.

CHAPTER 3

ADRIAN RODE HIS HORSE FOR over a mile before he began to circle back.

He came up behind the house, staying in the woods and out of sight. The vegetable plot lay between him and the house, and all of the girls, including Lila and Rita, were out pulling weeds and killing insects. Adrian wasn't concerned that the girls would have to work, that would be the case wherever they went. He was concerned because of the lack of calluses on Reggie's hands and the expressions he thought he'd seen on the other girls' faces.

Something wasn't right. Maybe they beat the girls. Whatever it was, he wasn't leaving Lila and Rita until he was sure they would be safe.

As he watched, Reggie sat on an upturned bucket in the shade, leaning his back against a tree. He wasn't working a bit, and in Adrian's now suspicious mind he appeared to be more of a guard than a protector, as though there was a risk of one or more of the girls running away. *Still, I don't have anything stronger than a hunch. I need to wait for something real before deciding anything.*

Adrian settled in comfortably and watched for the rest of the afternoon. There was a bucket of water next to Reggie. Occasionally one of the girls would raise her hand and ask permission to drink, waiting for Reggie to nod before walking over and getting a dipper of water. On two occasions, a girl would raise her hand with two fingers extended, obviously signaling a need for a sanitary break. Reggie would nod and the girl would walk to the out-house between the food plot and the main house.

There was no chattering among the girls.

Adrian thought that extraordinary. In his experience girls always talked to each other, no matter what they were doing. These girls were completely silent. More than anything, Adrian had seen or heard, this was the most ominous sign that these girls were being treated as prisoners, perhaps as slaves. As the sun slowly settled to the horizon, Adrian began getting a sick feeling in his stomach. He didn't like where his thoughts were going, yet he had nothing much other than some odd—or possibly imagined—facial expressions, a lack of chatter, and a lazy man to go by. He needed a lot more than that. So far he had not seen any actual mistreatment of the girls. The worst he could say was that Lacy and Reggie were apparently both lazy and strict.

A little before sunset, Reggie stood and waved his hands at the girls in a shooing motion. The girls all stood, dusted themselves off, and started walking to the house, Reggie following behind. Adrian watched as the girls filed in the back door and waited for Reggie to enter and close it behind him. He then moved up closer but stayed in the brush. He would need the cover of full darkness to get closer to the house, in case anyone decided to use the outhouse. He didn't think he would be able to see in through the windows, they were too heavily curtained—another ominous sign now that he thought about it. But he hoped he might be able to hear conversation if he got close to the windows.

Adrian spotted a long wooden ladder on the ground next to the back wall; it might be useful at some point in the night.

An hour went by before it was dark enough. If anyone came out now, they would be carrying a lantern, and wouldn't be able to see past its small circle of light. He could remain hidden easily. He silently walked beneath all of the windows but heard nothing from any of them. He then moved around the end of the house and stopped by the front corner. The entry had a lantern hanging from the porch rafters. Since there was no one outside to need the lantern, Adrian believed it was a signal, and his worst fears came that much closer to being confirmed.

As he was considering getting the ladder and trying to see or hear through the upper windows he saw a lantern bobbing in the distance. Soon he heard voices, and then two men came into sight, each carrying a burlap bag filled with something. They stepped up onto the porch and knocked. Almost immediately the door opened and the two men went inside, the door shutting behind them.

Where Adrian had been taking his time, with the arrival of these two men, he knew time was now short and he had to get into action. He ran back around the house to the ladder, set it up under the upper floor window furthest from the outhouse, and climbed the ladder rapidly and looked and listened. No sign of light or sound. He tried to open the window, but it was locked.

Taking a chance on giving himself away, he knocked out a pane of glass with the handle of his knife. Within seconds for he was inside the room. It was a bedroom containing a made bed, a chair, a night stand with a washing bowl, a mirror and a pitcher of water. The room was ready to be used, but obviously wasn't a room one of the girls occupied.

Adrian eased open the door.

The corridor was dark. He stepped into the corridor, finding himself near the end of it. It was pitch dark all the way to the stairwell.

Faint light came up the stair well, and the sounds of distant conversation. He couldn't make out the words but he heard a man's laughter clearly enough. *Probably one of the two I saw come in. Reggie doesn't seem the type to laugh. Lord...If I'm wrong about what's going on here I'll be sorely embarrassed. But better to be embarrassed than leave the girls here without checking.*

As he waited, the voices grew louder. Then he heard a girl's voice. Although he couldn't make out her words, the tone was sullen and resigned.

He stayed where he was. Soon there was a light coming up the stairwell and the sound of footsteps. One set heavy, one light. Adrian moved back into the room and closed the door to a slit, watching to see who was coming upstairs.

It was one of the men he had seen come in a few minutes before, and the oldest girl, the one who had made the face.

The man held her wrist and pulled her along. She resisted to a minor extent, but was not defiant. It looked to Adrian as though she was about to do something she didn't want to do, but was afraid not to for fear of something even worse.

Adrian eased his door completely closed. He watched and listened as the footsteps indicated that the pair had stopped short of the room he was in. Had they come into this room Adrian would have had to act immediately, and with less evidence for his actions. *But enough evidence.*

He waited and heard a door farther up the corridor open and close. Adrian eased his door open. The corridor was empty and dark, but lantern light showed dimly from under the second door from the stairs. Adrian waited another moment, then he soft-stepped down the hall and placed his ear against the door of the occupied room.

He heard the man talking roughly to the girl, telling her to "get out of those things right now" then the sound of a slap.

Slowly Adrian turned the door knob—it was unlocked.

Adrian shoved the door open and stood, taking in the tableau. The man, his shirt half unbuttoned, was staring at Adrian with a look halfway between confusion and anger. The girl was already stripped to her bra and underpants. She had a red welt on her face where the man had slapped her. Then the man spoke, "Get out of here shithead! This is my room and my girl, bought and paid for. Get out!"

Adrian ignored the man and looked at the girl. "He hit you?" She nodded yes, her eyes large and frightened. "He pay for you?" She nodded again, this time with shame, and looked down, slowly bringing her hands up to try to cover herself. "This what you want?" Adrian asked. This time she shook her head rapidly back and forth.

Adrian turned his attention back to the man, who had by now was furious. He began moving towards Adrian in a hostile manner. Adrian asked bitterly, "You in the habit of raping young girls, are you?"

Adrian's tone of voice, the look on his face, and the man's gradual realization that Adrian was so big he filled the door frame, made the man stop in his tracks. "I paid, it's not rape."

Adrian looked at him with disgust for a long moment. "I'll not argue with you, you already know you're wrong. How long you been coming here?" Adrian's voice was low and hard.

The man, knowing he would not stand a chance fighting Adrian, and knowing he was in the wrong, answered with fear and some shame. "Few months. They been here a couple years I think, but I just moved into the area a few months ago."

"Lot of men come here?"

"It gets pretty busy some nights, yeah." He said almost defiantly.

"What about the little girls?"

"They cost too much. I can't afford the amount of trade goods they cost."

Adrian stared at the man while the full import of the man's words sank in. Then the look on Adrian's face shifted to extreme loathing.

Jumping forward without warning, Adrian grabbed the man's right arm and twisted before the man had a chance to move. Adrian twisted until the shoulder popped out of its socket. The man gasped then began to scream in fear and pain. Adrian balled up a fist and slugged the man in the solar plexus, audibly driving the air from his lungs and temporarily paralyzing the diaphragm muscle. The scream died immediately. Adrian grabbed the right arm again and effortlessly broke it at the elbow, making the man a cripple for life. The man passed out. Adrian carelessly dropped him to the floor.

The girl stood stiff in shock. The violence had lasted less than two seconds, but was all the more brutal for its swiftness. She had never seen a man as big as Adrian in as ugly a mood as he was. She had never seen anyone move that fast. The only half formed thought in her mind was that the man on the floor was lucky to be alive.

Adrian raised his eyes from the man on the floor to the girl. She revised her thought. He was lucky to be in one piece much less alive. The look on Adrian's face was terrifying, even though she knew it wasn't aimed at her. This man who had sat across the dinner table from her earlier, this famous man that had looked big and gentle, now looked anything but gentle. He looked like he could and would kill anyone he saw. He reminded her of the description she had once read of a Viking Berserker, a man that had become something different from a man, a killing machine filled with unrepressed rage. She started shaking, hard. This wasn't the man at lunch earlier, this was that man's body possessed by wild, blood-thirsty, demons.

Adrian instructed her, "Run down stairs screaming. Don't say anything, just keep pointing up the stairs. Make all the noise you can, but no actual words. Act like you're more frightened than you've ever been in your life, like you've seen something too horrible to describe. I want Lacy and Reggie to come running up here. Can you do that for me?"

The girl nodded mutely. Could she do that? Hell yes she could do that, and acting wasn't going to be required. She'd do anything this man asked after he had rescued her, even if he was a devil-man. The girl took off running for the stairs. Adrian dragged the man's unconscious body across the room, propping it into a sitting position beneath the window. He closed the door, then stood where he would be behind it when it opened, and waited.

He didn't have to wait long.

He heard the girl downstairs, screaming like she was being gutted. *She sure can put on an act.* Then a long silence. Footsteps coming up the stairs, two sets. Footsteps coming down the hall, a bit reluctantly. Slowly the door opened, swinging to cover Adrian.

Reggie came in first, a pistol in-hand. Upon spotting the man against the far wall and the gruesome angles of his broken right arm, Reggie gasped and stopped. Lacy moved around him to see, and she suddenly stopped also.

Adrian hit the door hard and it shut with a loud bang. Reggie and Lacy jumped and spun around, fear on their faces, eyes bulging and their skin whitened by shock. As soon as Reggie saw Adrian, he began to raise the pistol towards him. Adrian leaped forward, slapping the gun hand to the side, plunging his knife into Reggie's throat. Ripping the knife out sideways, he cut Reggie's head almost halfway off.

The pistol fell to the floor, then Reggie fell and

began thrashing around, spraying blood all over as he tried to slow the bleeding with his hands. Reggie's face was rigid with extreme shock and terror, his mouth moving as though to form words, words that there was no air to form.

While Adrian's attention was on Reggie, Lacy pulled a razor-sharp filet knife from the folds of her dress and slashed at Adrian. He pulled back just in time, and what might have been a fatal blow became a shallow cut across his collar bone. As he stepped closer to slap the knife from her hand, Adrian slipped in Reggie's blood, giving Lacy the chance to make another stab at Adrian, this time aiming at his groin.

Adrian blocked the knife, then grabbed her by the wrist and slung her out and away from him. Lacy flew across the room, hitting the far wall and bouncing off it, landing on the floor in a heap.

Adrian watched as she slowly stood, then turned toward Adrian, the knife handle protruding from her chest. She stared at Adrian for a second, her eyes not seeing him. Then she settled down into a sitting position, almost as if her legs had melted from beneath her. She died sitting up.

Adrian looked around the dimly-lit, blood-splattered room. Reggie was dead, lying on the floor. The "customer" was unconscious, his arm mangled. Lacy was still sitting up, her bones and muscles holding up her lifeless body in precarious balance. *That fella is going to wake up to one hell of a gruesome scene, and in his own extreme pain. Son of a bitch deserves every bit of the pain, too.*

Using a clean towel and the wash-basin Adrian

rapidly washed the blood off his face and arms as much as he could before heading down the stairs. As he stepped into the hallway, the other "customer" was cautiously coming up the stairwell. He saw Adrian and stopped, then suddenly turned and ran down the stairs and out the front door. Adrian never saw him again.

Descending the stairs he saw the girls. Many of them were huddled around the oldest girl. They all looked frightened.

Rita and Lila came running up to Adrian as soon as they recognized him, but even they stopped a few feet short of him and stared.

His clothes were sprayed with fresh, dark, red blood. His face and arms were mostly clear of blood, except for the cut across his collar bone that was bleeding freely. But it was his face that stopped them. He wore an expression that, as Lila would later say, *"Would've scared the Grim Reaper into taking a dirt road."*

Then Lila came up to him, looked at the cut and said, "We need to get something on that cut, it's pretty deep."

Adrian looked at her hard, as though he didn't recognize her, then he looked around the room at sixteen scared girls staring back at him, sixteen girls that he just that moment realized were now his responsibility, and said, "Aw shit," then he sat down in the nearest chair.

He had accidentally rescued two girls, tried to get rid of them and wound up with fourteen more.

"Aw shit!" he said again.

CHAPTER 4

HE OLDEST GIRL, RACY, WAS seventeen. She quickly took charge of the situation.

"Lorna, bring that lantern in off the porch and lock the door. Gina, you and Tracy get some water boiling, some clean cloths and the sewing kit. Erin, you take charge of the rest of the girls and get dinner started. All of you change out of those whore clothes as soon as you can, start packing up to travel. You'll need to pack light, so pack practical clothes, wear your best walking shoes. We'll need every bit of food in the house. Get moving now!"

The girls all responded quickly to Racy's orders, even Lila and Rita jumped to obey. Adrian sat in the chair, watching with a vacant look. All he could think of was, *Sixteen girls. My God what am I going to do with sixteen girls. I can't leave them on their own, that wouldn't be right. They can't stay here, there'll be too many former "customers" that won't leave them alone. Sixteen girls, holy shit.*

He saw the girls moving around briskly, but he hadn't been paying attention and had no idea what they were doing, and at the moment didn't care. *I was just minding my own damn business, taking a nice little trip to Corpus Christi, and then WHAM! Sixteen girls. What the hell am I going to do now?*

Adrian sat like that for several more minutes, lost in his own thoughts, wondering what he was going to do with all these girls when Racy told him to stand up and follow her into the kitchen. Adrian followed her instructions mechanically, his subconscious mind responding while his conscious mind was in a state of shock, and not from the brief violence upstairs.

Racy sat him down at the table where the light was best, then began cleaning his wound. With a businesslike efficiency and workmanlike fingers, she soon had the knife cut sewed up and bandaged.

Racy had been in charge of the girls for so long it was second nature to her. She had nursed them through sickness, doctored their wounds, held their hands and been a nurse and surrogate mother for two years, ever since Jane had died and left Racy as the oldest. Adrian sat through her ministrations without flinching, or acknowledging she was in the room.

"There Mr. Hunter," she said. "You're all fixed up now. Is there any point in my going upstairs?"

Adrian, forced by her direct question into responding said, "No, no reason at all. Lacy and Reggie are dead, the other man has a badly broken arm. When he comes to he won't pose a problem for anyone, he'll be in too much pain. Just let him leave the way he is, don't try to fix his arm. Son of a bitch deserves a lot more pain than that. On the other hand, you might run up there and fetch Reggie's pistol, don't want to leave that where he can find it when he wakes up."

Racy went up the stairs and spotted the open

door with light coming from the room. She stopped on the threshold, aghast at the carnage and the creepy site of Lacy sitting on her heels but dead. She suddenly had a mounting fear of Adrian. Had she seen this room first, she might not have been so cavalier at ordering him around and stitching him up. She had been amazed that while stitching him he had shown no signs of pain.

After seeing this room she now thought that was a bit of a minor point.

Racy took a deep breath, then walked into the room, carefully stepping around the various pools of blood and retrieved the pistol.

When she returned downstairs Adrian was sitting just as she had left him. She laid the pistol on the table next to him and diffidently asked "What do you want me to do next?"

"Yeah, that's the question isn't it? I've been thinking about that. What do I do next? I can't go off and leave you girls here. You might be able to feed yourselves, but you won't be able to protect yourselves. You could probably fight off one or two men, maybe even half a dozen. But sooner or later there will be a group of men that you can't fight off, and your odds of ending back up in this situation... or worse...are too high for comfort."

"How in hell do I take you with me though? And where can I leave you off? I didn't plan on keeping Rita and Lila to raise, I'm sure not planning on raising sixteen girls. Good Lord what a fubar this is. Can't take you with me, can't leave you behind, and probably never find a safe place to leave you." Adrian looked directly at Racy, seeming to seeing her for the first time. "Thank you for sewing me up, I appreciate it."

"You said you were going to Corpus Christi, why not take us with you? It'll be slower with all of us walking, and the young ones not able to walk fast, but we'll get there eventually and unless you have some reason to rush then why not? Eating will be the biggest problem on the trip. Takes a lot of food for this many girls you know, and the food we have will be hard to carry. There's lots of food in the pantry and store room—mostly what the men traded for us. There're quite a few guns and lots of bullets, too; that was another favorite trade item. Reggie traded us for whatever he thought he could trade again and gain on. People stopped by here not just to take a girl upstairs but often just to trade. If we could find a wagon of some kind, we could carry most of it with us. Take two wagons probably to carry it all."

Adrian perked up a little at hearing this news. "That might be an idea...if there's enough valuables here, and if we can carry them with us, then we might be able to find a place for you in Corpus, a safe place maybe since the Navy is down there. Oh crap, what am I thinking? Sailors and girls? That doesn't sound safe."

"We can handle a lot more than you might think. We won't be safe here—I agree with you on that,— maybe we'll be okay in Corpus Christi, and maybe we won't. We won't know until we get there and look it over. We might as well check it out though don't you think?"

As she talked, Racy noticed how normal Adrian was acting now, more or less as he had at dinner.

It was hard to reconcile the mayhem she had seen upstairs and the fierceness of the man as he had descended the stairs with this seemingly gentle giant whose biggest concern seemed to be what to do with the sixteen girls on his hands.

She looked him over carefully; her life might well depend on him for some time to come. He was, she noted, very tall, maybe six-five, and as handsome as any man she had ever seen, but in a rough kind of way. He was heavily muscled, and she would bet his weight was somewhere around two-hundred-seventy or more, but no fat. He had a large scar that ran from the lower portion of his cheek, on down his neck and into his shirt, the scar he had gotten from fighting a grizzly bear in the Colorado mountains. She knew this from the stories that circulated about him. He was famous after all—the most famous man since the grid had dropped. She'd heard all the stories.

A massive coronal mass ejection had destroyed the electric grids worldwide four years previously, and civilization had come to an abrupt end. But Adrian Hunter was one of those men whose exploits had spread, first by ham radio, and then by word of mouth. Only the most reclusive and isolated of people hadn't heard of "General Bear," as he was known. Even some of them must have heard the stories of his breeding with a grizzly bear and having cubs all over the Colorado mountains, or speculated over the news of his semi-engagement to Colonel Linda Hunter. Those kinds of stories spread far and fast.

"Racy...is that your real name?"

"You mean is that my real name or my 'working name'?" she asked with sudden anger.

"Well, yeah. I guess you got me there. I didn't want to insult you by calling you something you didn't like. Maybe I was a bit heavy handed in asking, but I didn't mean it as an insult."

"Oh...I'm sorry. It was nice of you to ask." Her sudden anger faded as quickly as it had come. "I didn't want to be a prostitute, don't ever want to be one again either. I was forced into it, beaten into unconsciousness several times. After being raped so many times that I lost count I just quit resisting. My real name is Rachel, but my family used to call me Racy because when I was little I ran really fast everywhere I went. I'll keep the name, thank you."

"Okay Racy, do you have any idea where we might get some wagons as you suggested?"

"Wagons? No, not really. But I know where there's a big truck that runs on wood, and it belongs to a son of a bitch that I'm going to kill before we leave. He's one of the most frequent customers, and the roughest. It's not far from here. Let me have that pistol and I'll go get it."

"I beg your pardon?"

Racy repeated patiently, "Let me have the pistol and I'll go get the truck. I think it will carry all the valuables and all the girls—and no walking will be needed. We can get to Corpus a lot faster."

"You planning on just driving the truck off, or do you plan on killing its owner first? Or maybe you plan to take him hostage and make him drive it?"

Racy's voice was serious. "I plan on killing him first. I plan on killing him regardless of the truck. I'm not leaving here with him alive, on foot or by truck or by any means there is. I aim to kill him, he's got it coming, just ask any of the girls."

"Is there anyone else on your list or is he the only one?"

"There would be plenty more, but I don't know where they are. I know where this one is and he was the worst of the bunch. Once I kill him, I can take the truck, and whatever else he has worth taking. Since he uses the truck to go out trading and scavenging he probably has a lot of good stuff."

Adrian studied her face for a long moment. She was dead serious, she wasn't joking around. Adrian smiled a little, for the first time all day. "Racy, I believe you would do just as you say. Trouble is you might be overloading yourself. Maybe you could kill him, but then maybe he won't die so easy. You thought about that?"

"Thought about it? I've been thinking about it for two years Mr. Hunter. It's a thought that has kept me going on many a night. I have thought about it, planned it, visualized it, dreamed of it and swore myself to do it when the time came where I could. I am going to do it, it's as simple as that. He may be hard to kill, but I'll get six bullets into him no matter what else happens, or what may happen to me. Using Reggie's gun just adds a bit of irony to it."

Adrian was blown away by Racy's fervor. Yet, not only could he understand it, he agreed with her. She had this to do, and needed to do it. Even though she wasn't grown up yet, she had some serious payback due to her. She had a lot of scores to settle, and this might be the only one she would ever have a chance to see through.

Adrian decided to help her.

"Racy, why don't you get the girls started packing,

keep them busy. Tell them you and I will be gone for a while. I probably shouldn't do this, but I'll help you settle up and then we'll get his truck."

"First," she said, with infinite patience, "I already have the girls busy packing; you weren't paying attention earlier. Second, this is mine to do, not yours. I will not be cheated of this by you or anyone else. I'll kill him, no one else."

"Understood, I'll just go along to back you up. It'll be your show. Plus, do you know how to operate the wood burner and drive the truck? I do. Besides, I won't let you go alone, either I go or you don't go at all."

Racy folded her arms and studied him for a moment, then nodded quickly. "Yes sir. When do you want to leave?"

"Why not right now? How far is it?"

"Half an hour or so. I'll change clothes and be right back."

While she was gone Adrian took a moment to tell Lila and Rita and the rest of the girls that he and Racy were going to get a truck and would be back in a few hours, and to mind the next oldest girl while they were gone. He had no sooner finished talking to them, than Racy was back. She was dressed in jeans and boots and a plaid shirt, with a light jacket. She already had Reggie's pistol in her jacket pocket. She was impatient to get going.

CHAPTER 5

"**C**OME ON MR. HUNTER!" SAID Racy. "The girls will be fine. I gave shotguns to the two oldest girls, they know how to use them. And I gave them a password for when we come back or they might use them on us. We'll only be gone a little while. Let's get going."

Adrian studied her in silence. *She really wants to kill this guy bad. He must be a real piece of shit, 'cause she seems like a nice enough girl otherwise. Maybe she's psycho, but she doesn't act like it—other than this one thing.* "Okay, let's get."

The moon had crested the tree tops and shed enough light that a lantern wasn't necessary. As they walked Adrian asked, "You ever kill anyone before?"

"Why?"

"Seems like a pertinent question given what you're up to doesn't it?"

"Yes. I mean yes it's a pertinent question. No, I've never killed anyone before."

"Are you totally sure this is what you want to do? A lot of people spend the rest of their lives regretting killing someone, even though they thought it was a good idea at the time."

"I don't know if it's the right thing to do or not." Racy replied. "I don't know if I'll regret it the rest of my life, but I doubt it very much. I do know that I'll regret *not* killing him for the rest of my life if I don't. He'll find some other girls to rape, and he likes them young Mr. Hunter, real young."

"How about you call me Adrian. 'Mr. Hunter' seems a bit formal, given the circumstances. I can't recall the last time I helped a young girl commit murder. How old are you anyway?"

"Seventeen, Adrian. And it's not murder, its justice. It's not the formal, legal kind of justice, its real justice. The kind you can only get for yourself. If you're having second thoughts you can go on back."

Adrian laughed out loud. "Go back, no I don't think so. I'm not having second thoughts...I just want to be sure *you* don't have second thoughts after it's too late to change anything." He pointed ahead of them. "I see a lit window up ahead, is that his house?"

"That's it. That's where that sick rat-bastard Charley lives."

"Do you have a plan? You said you have planned this out. What are the details?"

"I've thought it over a thousand times," she said, never looking away from the house. "Here's my plan: I look in the windows to see if he's alone. From all I've gathered, he lives alone so he most likely will be. If he has company, I wait until they leave or go to sleep. Then I knock on the door. When Charley answers, I shoot him. Six times with this pistol. It's simple and should work. The key will be for me not to hesitate to shoot. No fancy speeches, or talking at all. No long stares. Soon as the door is clear enough to hit him I start shooting. If he doesn't drop right there, I run. How's that sound?"

"I like it. You're right, it's simple and it should work. You've spotted the weak spots and accounted for them. Now it's just a matter of actually doing it. I'll stand back behind you a little ways. If things go bad, just drop and lay down flat to give me a clear field of fire. Knowing I'm there and ready to help should steady your nerves some and make it a bit more sure that you'll do it right." He paused for just a moment, then continued. "Are you sure you're not going to say something to him first?"

"God, would I love to. I'd love to preach to him for an hour before pulling the trigger. I dreamed of making him get on his knees and beg. But, he's cagy. If I don't start shooting right off when he opens that door, he'll know something is up, slam the door and get his own gun, if he doesn't come to the door with one in his hand already. Talking to him would be satisfying, but it's not necessary. He already knows he's an asshole, telling him he's one won't make any difference. Killing him will make a difference. I'm going to look into the windows now. Wait here."

Adrian waited, bemused by being ordered around by a seventeen year-old girl bent on committing murder. He watched her sneak up to the house and peek in through the windows. She was careful not to stick her head in front of any of the windows. She stood to the side of each one, looked in as far as she could from the side angle, ducked under and came up the other side and looked again. Then she swiftly came back to Adrian.

"He's alone. He's sitting in front of the fire, drinking. He looks like he's about to fall asleep. Now's the time. Stay back and don't interfere—please."

"Okay. Say, how sure are you that pistol is going to fire?"

"You must think I'm and idiot. I've seen it fire, I know it works. I checked the loads, it has six live rounds in it. It's a double action; all I have to do is aim and pull the trigger. One of the reasons I'm using it is because I've seen it shot and know it'll shoot. Geez, Adrian, give me *some* credit."

Without any sign of hesitation, Racy strode to the house, mounted the steps, walked across the porch, pulled the screen door back, and rapped sharply on the door. Then she raised the pistol to chest height, and aimed it at the side of the door where Charley would be standing when he opened the door, and waited.

After a moment, a man's voice came from inside the door "Who is it?" he called, but the door didn't open.

Adrian thought, *There went the plan, wonder what she'll do next.*

Racy called out in a loud voice, "Miss Lacy asked me to come fetch you. Seems we have a new girl for you, just got in today."

The door opened halfway, exposing most of Charley's body.

Bang, Bang, Bang, and Charlie fell across the threshold, half in and half out of the house.

Bang, Bang, Bang, each shot making the dead man's body jiggle a little from the bullet's impact. Her first shot hit him in the stomach, the second in the chest and the third in the head as he fell. He was dead before he hit the floor.

Then Racy started shouting and screaming at the

body. She called him every kind of name that Adrian had heard and some he hadn't. When she quit screaming she started kicking the body as viciously as she could. Adrian watched with concern. He didn't want her to hurt her foot kicking it, and then not be able to walk. She would be something of a burden if that happened.

It didn't occur to him to think her behavior strange or odd, or even wrong. This man had raped her repeatedly, had raped her friends repeatedly. He deserved to die and she deserved to be the one to kill him. Venting her rage now seemed normal to him and he was going to let her vent until she was exhausted.

It was what she needed. He respected that.

But he didn't want her to cripple herself either, so he looked around and found a shovel leaning against the fence. He took that and, grabbing her arm, put the shovel in her hands,

"Hit him with this, save your feet for walking."

He stood back while she whaled on the body with the shovel. Eventually she slowed and then stopped, leaning on the shovel and taking great, rasping breaths.

Four years ago this would have been unthinkable. Had it happened, it would have been an international news sensation. But four years ago was a long time ago, another world entirely. When electricity stopped so did everything else. No electricity meant no heat, no water, no food deliveries, money useless, and no fuel to run anything. Ninety-seven percent of Americans died in the first two years from starvation, disease and exposure. There were masses of suicides and murders as well. Those few that did survive had to be extremely tough, extremely adaptable, able to produce or procure their own food, ruthless in protecting themselves. This girl was a survivor, what she was doing now was hard, but right. Whether it would have been right four years ago is moot, fact is, it's right for these times.

"You done, or just taking a break?" Adrian asked in an amused voice.

"I'm done."

"You sure? I don't want to deprive you of any justice you got coming."

"Are you making fun of me?"

"I don't make fun of people that just killed a man in cold blood then beat the shit out of his corpse with a shovel. Making fun of people like that isn't smart. But I am curious if you're done so we can find the truck and get back to the girls. I don't like leaving them alone this long."

"Okay, I'm done. Let's find that truck. You look around for it; it has to be close by. I'll look inside the house and see what he has worth taking."

"You have any more bullets for that pistol?"

"No sir. I used them up and didn't think to bring more."

"Take my pistol. You know how to use it?"

She looked it over and said, "Yes sir, I do." My daddy had one of these, a 1911 he called it. Taught me how to shoot it.

"All right, take it, check out the house. I'll find the truck and holler at you from the porch if you're still inside."

Adrian found the truck in a carriage shed behind

the house. It was a two-and-a-half ton. Adrian recognized it from his army days—they called it a deuce-and-a-half back then. It had a multi-fuel engine, which meant it could run on gasoline, diesel, kerosene, jet-fuel, even alcohol. It could be converted to run on natural gas easily. Someone had installed a wood gas generator in the back of the truck, similar to the ones Matthew, a blacksmith and preacher, was building back at Adrian's home, Fort Brazos, for trade.

The wood gas generator was sort of like a large double cooker. It consisted of a container that held wood, in this case made from a water heater tank. Below that you built a fire that heated the wood inside the tank. As the wood heated it released carbon gasses that were captured by a tube welded to the tank's removable top and led into another small closed tank full of water. The water cleaned the gas of most of the tars in the fumes before piping it to the engine's intake. Elegantly simple, wood gas generators had been used during WWII by farmers and other rural people when fuel had been strictly rationed. The US government had even printed a pamphlet on how to make them back during the war.

Adrian checked the wood tank, it was full. He started the fire, then went back to the house. As he arrived Racy was coming back out. She stepped over the body in the doorway without a glance.

She looked exhausted. *She should be exhausted. It's after midnight and she probably got up well before daylight and went to work in the kitchen making breakfast. Then a full day's work out in the field, and then this. If she isn't physically exhausted she must be emotionally exhausted.*

"There's a ton of stuff in here," she said. "All kinds of food. Bunch of guns and ammo. Enough for a small army."

"Start hauling it all out onto the porch" Adrian said. "I'll bring the truck around as soon as I can get it fired up, then we'll load up and go."

"I found bullets that fit Reggie's pistol. I reloaded; you can have your pistol back now."

"Thanks. You okay?"

"Sure, I'm okay. Help me drag his body out of the doorway though, would you?"

After they had dragged the body out the way, Adrian returned to the truck to check on the fire. Before he had gone ten feet he heard a yelp from Racy in the living room. Adrian spun on his heels and rushed back to the house.

CHAPTER 6

RACY WAS POINTING THE PISTOL at Bear.
"Whoa! Don't Shoot!" Adrian yelled at Racy. "That's my wolf, he won't hurt you. He followed us."

"Shit, Adrian! He scared the crap out of me! I've never seen anything like him before. I sure didn't see him following us."

"Well he doesn't follow right behind like a regular dog. He generally stays way off to the side where he can't be seen. He moves ahead now and then checking for bad guys. If he finds any he lets me see him; if I don't see him, it's good news and clear sailing. Sorry, forgot to tell you about him."

"I didn't hear him come in, I just turned around and there he was, staring at me."

"He won't hurt you. He's seen me being friendly with you, so he knows you're not an enemy. Unusual of him to come into the house after you like that though, he generally stays outside. He must like you quite a bit to come in like this. But don't try to pet him, he doesn't like it. You can talk to him, throw him scraps of food now and then, but don't hand him food—you might lose a finger. He's a wild animal, a full-blooded wolf that I found as a puppy and raised up. He's not my pet, he's my companion, but only as long as he wants it that way. He can leave whenever he wants to, and sometimes does for a day or two. Someday he'll get tired of me and go back to the wilds; until then he's a valued friend."

"You talk about him like he's human or something."

"He's not human, but he's smarter than some humans I've known, uncanny smart. Seems to understand most of what I say, and I haven't spent one second on trying to train him. What he knows, he just knows. Watch—Bear, guard the house."

Bear ran out the door and disappeared into the darkness. "He'll be out there somewhere watching the house. Anyone tries to approach, Bear will let me know about it. There won't be anyone sneaking past him."

Adrian went back to the garage and stoked the fire until he could hear the wood gas bubbling through the water in the cleaning chamber. The deuce-and-a-half was military-issue and didn't have an ignition key. He turned the starter and the truck engine tried to turn over. Engines were slow to start on wood gas and the battery sounded a little weak, so he shut it off. Looking around, he found a case of starting fluid. He put the case of cans in the back and used one to spray a little into the air intake. Then he started the engine again. This time it caught right away, then slowed down a bit as it began cycling on the wood gas.

While the engine warmed up, Adrian checked the tires on a horse trailer he'd spotted near the shed. They were still sound, but the truck's trailer hitch didn't fit, so he went back into the carriage shed and brought out a piece of chain he had noticed earlier which he used to make a crude, but effective, connection to pull the trailer.

By the time he pulled up to the front porch of the house, Racy had already put a large pile of supplies on the porch. *This girl isn't lazy.* With Adrian helping, it only took a few minutes to carry the rest of the goods out of the house and load everything onto the truck. It was quite a cache. Mostly canned goods, but there were some usable dry goods and several cases of canned meat and other dehydrated foods, enough to feed one person for a couple of years. Enough to feed the girls for quite a while.

By current standards, Charley had been a wealthy man. Racy had been right when she'd said he was a successful trader.

They loaded up twenty-seven rifles, fifteen handguns, and dozens of boxes of assorted ammunition. There were no two guns exactly alike in the whole bunch, but there seemed to be plenty of ammo for most of them. The guns could be traded for enough food to last them a couple of more years.

Quite a dowry. At least they're not going into the world as beggars. Poor kids deserved all this and more. They're not stealing—they're taking what's theirs, but not nearly enough of it.

As they finished loading up, Racy ran back into the house. She emerged a couple of minutes later, her expression flat.

"We better get going, the house will be burning like crazy in a minute."

Adrian pulled up to the girl's house and put the transmission in neutral, letting the engine run at idle while Racy went in to tell the girls to load all the food and guns they'd gathered along with their meager personal belongings.

With all they were carrying it was going to be a tight fit for the girls back there. He could squeeze in two of the smaller girls with him and Bear in the front, but that still left over a dozen in the back. With an eye to the future Adrian directed the girls to stack the boxes of food along the sides of the truck bed and across the back, making a wall all around the slatted wooden sides of the truck. He wanted the girls to be able to stay out of sight just in case they ran into a situation that called for it.

He also spent quite a bit of time coaxing Bear into the cab of the truck. Bear had run alongside as they returned, but that had been a relatively short distance. Adrian was planning on driving long distances each day. Bear would have to ride in the truck, and Bear had never been in a vehicle of any kind. Once Bear got the idea, he turned into a seat hog. That took more time to correct. When he finally had Bear situated, he loaded his horse into the horse trailer.

Most of the girls had packed by putting their belongings in the middle of a bed sheet and then gathering and tying the corners. One or two had suitcases. Each girl also had a bedroll consisting of two quilts and a pillow, with rain coats, winter coats, and towels rolled up inside. Racy had told the girls which pots and pans and dishes to pack into boxes, enough to prepare meals for everyone, and cleaning supplies for washing up, organizing the girls as well as any quartermaster sergeant; Adrian's opinion of her kept climbing.

"I'll ride in the back to keep an eye on the girls," she told Adrian. "If I need you to stop I'll bang on the cab window three times. If I bang more than three times you better look around and figure out what's wrong, because more than three means something is bad wrong, but there's too many things that could go wrong to have a signal for each of them. There are five girls I trust with a rifle. I'm going to set them each up with a loaded rifle, just in case. If the trouble is bad enough you may hear us shooting instead of me pounding on the cab."

Adrian simply nodded. *Seems Racy has taken charge of me, too.*

When Adrian didn't reply, Racy climbed into the back of the truck. After a moment, she yelled, "We're ready when you are!"

Two hours before daylight Adrian pulled away from the house. He was halfway surprised that Racy hadn't set it on fire too. As he drove off he looked back in the rear-view mirror and saw flames eating at the dark window coverings. *Girl's a regular arsonist. I sure don't want to get on her bad side. If that son of a bitch with the broken arm doesn't wake up soon and get out he'll burn to death. Bastard deserves it.*

Adrian stopped the truck, opened the door and leaned out "Racy, did you see if the guy upstairs was still there before you set the fire?" he called.

"He left before we got back. Wouldn't of mattered to me though."

Adrian closed the truck door without a word and drove off again. *Nope, don't want to get on her bad side.*

Adrian drove until the engine started to sputter from lack of wood gas. He pulled off the road, then shifted into all-wheel drive and slowly drove well back into the trees. There he shut the engine down. The sudden stillness and silence was a relief, although he hadn't realized until that moment that how loud it was.

Adrian opened the cab door and stepped out. He stood and stretched as high as he could, his arms reaching up and his back bowing as he got to his tip toes. A shudder of a muscle spasm ran down his body as his muscles almost groaned with relief at having movement again.

Racy came around from the back of the truck, rubbing her eyes. "Why'd we stop? Everything okay?"

"Time for a break, and we need to gather more wood for the gas generator. Tell the girls we need all the wood we can put in the back. Small pieces that will fit in the generator tank." He pointed back the way they'd come. "The road is that way, tell the girls to stay out of sight of it, and to keep the noise down. Don't want to alert anyone nearby any more than we already may have. We'll stay here for a couple of hours. Wouldn't be a bad idea to fix up a quick meal too. Then we'll get back on the road."

Adrian called Bear out of the cab and said "Wait here." Turning back to Racy he said, "Bring the girls by to meet Bear. I want Bear to get the idea they are not enemy, and for the girls to understand the same thing about him, that he's no enemy to them. While you make introductions, I'm going to take the horse out and water him, then walk around a little out there. Don't let any of the girls shoot me, okay?"

"Okay."

"Oh, and tell Bear to come find me when he's met all the girls. Just tell him to 'find Adrian.'"

An hour later Adrian came back to the truck, Bear stayed out on the perimeter. Adrian moved the horse to a spot where he could graze and hobbled him, leaving a bucket of water nearby. He found all of the girls sitting around a fire, eating. Adrian sat down with them and one of the girls handed him a plate that had already been prepared and waiting. Adrian took his time eating, thinking the situation they were in over bit by bit. When he finished his plate he said, "Good food, whoever prepared it did a good job. Thank you."

"Ladies, it's time for me to learn all of your names, get a little of each of your history, and to answer questions about myself. We're going to be together for a while, let's get comfortable with each other. First let me tell you my plan for you girls, see what you think of it. I'm pretty sure that's on the top of your minds right now, isn't it?"

Almost every girl nodded their heads up and down, some saying quietly, "Yes, sir."

Adrian rubbed a hand across his forehead. "Ladies, I am at a bit of a loss how to act here. I've not been around young girls before, and I don't know how to treat you. If you were boys, I think I'd be fine, but...obviously you're not. Here's what I need to know: How do you want me to treat you, and in return have you give me your instant obedience to any order I give you? It's not that I want to boss you around, but if we get into a bad situation, I need you to do exactly what I say and when I say it, without hesitation or question. I don't want to yell at you like I would men or boys, but I don't want you standing up after I yell 'hit the dirt,' either. Does that make sense?"

When Adrian finished the girls all looked from him directly at Racy, expecting her to answer for them.

She looked at them one at a time, then turned to Adrian. "I think if you treat us the way you have so far, it'll be just fine. We've been treated like cattle for so long we've forgotten what being treated with respect feels like. I can't remember the last time anyone asked any of us our opinion about anything. You just did, and I think we are all in a bit of shock over it. We just kind of assumed that you would boss us around like everyone else has."

She looked around at the girls again before continuing. "In fact, I think we would all like to hear why you're helping us instead of either using us or abandoning us."

CHAPTER 7

ADRIAN CLEARED HIS THROAT. FINDING sixteen pairs of young girl's eyes glued to his every move and expression unnerved him. He cleared his throat again.

"I guess I don't see any choice in the matter. I don't think any decent man would have any better luck dealing with this than me. I would have left you behind if I thought you'd been able to take care of yourselves. Or if you had all been older and there voluntarily. But, I don't think you would have been okay for long, and you weren't there voluntarily. You were all there against your will, being raped. It sickens me that you've been put through that. Tell me, have all of you been raped?"

Racy replied, "Everyone that has had her period. Lacy watched for that, and as soon as it happened she put the girl up for auction. I guess we were lucky she waited that long. When we knew a girl had her first period, we hid it from Lacy as long as we could. Sometimes we could hide it for several months, but she always found out sooner or later."

Adrian nodded. "Okay, so here's the deal," he said. "One of these days you're going to run into people that will judge you, and consider you to be low-life's, even trash, because of having been prostituted. It won't matter to them that you were forced, that you were raped. Their little minds won't comprehend that you had no choice. Certainly they have no right to judge a girl for what she has been forced to do."

Adrian looked at each girl for a moment, locking eyes with them one at a time. Some of them blushed and looked down, some held his gaze. A couple held his gaze defiantly.

He continued, trying to be gentle, but firm. "When you're back around other people, it's up to you whether you bring up your past. You can talk about it, or not, as you personally see fit. But, if you don't want to talk about it you'll need a consistent cover story. If you don't want to discuss it, just say that you were in an orphanage for girls, that the head mistress died a week before I came by to drop off Rita and Lila, and that since there was no adult in charge I took you with me to find another place for you to live. Simple and effective, okay?"

Most of the girls nodded.

"But whether you choose to talk about it or not, you need to be prepared for the story to get out, for people to look at you differently. Some men will try to treat you poorly. Most men won't pay you much attention at all. Good men will treat you as the ladies that you are. It's the way life is, be ready to deal with it and remember that whatever may happen or may be said, you are no worse, or no better, than anyone else. You're just people too. Okay?"

Around the campfire, he watched the girls carefully. A few of them nodded, their heads barely moving.

"All right, now, back to answering your question. I couldn't leave you behind, because sooner or later the men that had been frequenting the place would return. I'll take you as far as Corpus Christi. I hope to find you a good house there and get you set up as a trading post. You've got a darned good start with what's in the back of the truck. By careful trading and sound negotiating you should be able to keep yourselves fed and clothed and sheltered. I'm going to teach you ladies how to defend yourselves as we travel. By the time we get to Corpus, I expect each of you—even the youngest ones—to be able to handle a gun expertly, to work together as a team. With luck and some hard training, I'll leave you there in excellent shape, and safe. Then I'll say goodbye and return to my travels. When I finish my trip, I'll come back and check in on you; and take anyone who wants to go back to Fort Brazos with me. Does that sound okay to all of you?"

Most of the girls nodded, the rest just stared at him, making him uncomfortable. Adrian had a prescient moment where he knew that when the time came to leave them behind he would feel like he was abandoning them, and that some of them would feel the same way. *But I didn't take them on to raise, and couldn't take care of them if I wanted to, without abandoning my own life, at least not until I can get them back home and set up somehow.*

"Okay then, let's get started teaching me your names. I want each of you to just call me Adrian. Racy, would you introduce them by age, starting with the youngest first?"

Racy stood and walked behind the girls. She

stopped behind each one and gave her name and a couple of brief words of their backgrounds, all of which were remarkably similar: orphans that had been taken in by guile and then used by Lacy and Reggie. "Gina, Tracy, Erin, Alana, Celia, Selena, Lena, Shayla, Victoria, Faye, Rylie, Helen and Regan. And you already know Lila and Rita." As each girl was introduced Adrian said hello and called her by name.

When the introductions were complete, Adrian said, "It'll take a while for me to get your names all straight, bear with me until I do." Then thinking that manners might be a good thing to show he added, "Please."

He stood up and stretched. "Let's get the wood collected and then get back on the road."

Racy spoke up. "Can I make a suggestion? It might be a good idea to stop here for the day, let everyone kind of get used to the idea that we're no longer slaves, that our lives are extremely different."

She must have seen the puzzled look on Adrian's face, because she continued quickly.

"I know this must sound crazy to you, Adrian, but this is the biggest day in our lives, ever. I'd like to see the girls play, that's something they haven't been allowed to do. Just loaf around and play. One day of that won't hurt, will it?"

Adrian scratched his head. *Play? They need to play? Oh geez what have I gotten into.* "I expect not Racy, one day isn't going to make a lot of difference. Go ahead and set up camp, get the girls situated and then let them play all day. I'll go hunting so you all can have privacy. When I come back you'll hear me whistling."

Adrian took off, collecting Bear outside the camp. He carried his M4 and went looking for wild hogs. Feral hogs had become a problem in Texas even before the grid dropped, reaching a critical mass of four-million with their population doubling every two years, in spite of intense hunting pressure. With few humans to restrict them in any way, the wild hog population had grown to numbers making them an important part of the food chain—hogs had become to the grid survivors in East Texas what the buffalo had been to the Plains Indians. Adrian was now traveling through heavily populated hog territory. With Bear to sniff them out, it didn't take long to find some.

Adrian shot two of the smaller hogs—young ones were better eating; easier to carry, clean, and cook; and there wouldn't be much, if any, waste. Seventeen people and a wolf could put a quick end to two young hogs. Adrian field dressed them, then tossed the internal organs to Bear while he tied the pig's feet together and slung them over his neck like a bandolier.

When he got close to the camp, he could hear the girls; they were laughing, giggling and apparently having a great time on their day off. He sat down to wait; there was still plenty of day left, and if they needed a day of fun, as Racy suggested, then he didn't want to put a damper on it or inhibit them with his presence. After three hours, they seemed to have settled. Adrian began walking towards them, whistling loudly.

The girls all looked up at him as he came into the camp. They did look more relaxed than they had before. Adrian gave them a big smile as he stood there with the two dead and gutted pigs hanging from his shoulders.

Racy said, "What's wrong with your face? Stop that!"

Rita spoke up, "He did that to us too—he thinks he's smiling."

All the girls started laughing and making strange faces at Adrian. Adrian started laughing, as much at himself as at the girl's antics.

When they finally settled down, he lifted the pigs off his shoulder. "I brought a couple of small pigs to cook, we'll eat fresh, hot, roasted pork tonight. We'll need two decent-sized fires, four forked sticks, and two long sticks for spits."

Lila asked Adrian, "Could you please cut their heads off before you cook them?"

"Sure thing Lila, sure thing."

That evening, after everyone had eaten their fill of the delicious meat, Adrian studied the girls. They were full, warm, and comfortable. They seemed to be at ease, he didn't see nearly as much signs of tension among them as before. He had noticed earlier that the girls seemed fascinated by his every move, even if it was just to scratch an itch, he invariably found over a dozen sets of eyes watching him. For a while it made him self-conscious, but after some thought he realized it was natural and tried to give it no more mind. They were wary of him because of the way men had treated them in the past.

"Ladies", he announced, "I think we'll stay here

another day, maybe even two. Tomorrow you can relax some more and enjoy our fine wild campsite. At noon, though, we're going to start training on guns and tactics. That means you'll learn how to march in step, how to move on patrol, how to take cover, and how to advance and cover. Eventually we'll get into ambush techniques, how to set them up and how to get out of them. We'll stop frequently on the way to practice. By the time we get to Corpus, you ladies will be as well-trained as any group of soldiers ever were. How does that sound?"

Racy replied, "Sounds great. It'll take us a while to get used to the idea, but I love it." With that endorsement, Adrian saw that the rest of the girls smiled. *Whatever Racy thinks is a good idea, the rest think is a good idea. They're so used to her being in charge that they have complete faith in her. She'll be the key to their survival.* "Race, I need you and two more girls to take turns with me on night watch. We'll each take two-hour turns at staying awake and being alert for any signs of danger. Might as well get used to it now, you'll all be doing it for years to come."

"*Race?* Adrian, I *like* that!" the tall girl said with a smile. "Thank you. Race it is from now on! Which watch will you take? I'll set the rest up."

"Last watch. Get me up two hours before sunrise, if I'm not already up, anyway. I'm a light sleeper, and with this many girls snoring I may not get any sleep at all." That started the girls giggling again, which spread to all the girls and quickly became hard laughter. Even Adrian was laughing *They act like escapees from a lunatic asylum. I guess it's the release of tension making them act silly.*

Race said, "Adrian, would you tell us about the bear cubs? We're all dying to know the real story, we know you didn't actually father bear cubs, but what *did* happen?"

"That story will haunt me to the day I die," Adrian said with a sigh. "I can't get away from it anywhere. Okay, here's what happened. My wife died a little over a year ago. She was pregnant at the time, although I didn't know it until after she had passed away. I was heartbroken and couldn't stand to stay where everything reminded me of her, so I left home and went to Colorado, to live in the mountains like a hermit. But as bad luck would have it I wasn't left alone. I hadn't been there long before I was attacked by a group of raiders—cannibals. I was more than half-crazy from grief and just wanted to be alone, so when they attacked me I went *full* crazy on them. One of them shot at me, and the bullet grazed my head."

Here Adrian pointed to the scar on the side of his head, pulling back the hair so they could see it.

"That gave me a concussion and I was in trouble. They were chasing me and I was getting real woozy, about to pass out. I found a hole up under a bunch of tree roots and crawled into it to hide, and then I did pass out. The men looking for me didn't find me. I was unconscious for several days. When I came to, I realized I was lying with my head on a hibernating bear's behind."

At this the girls giggled.

"It was a mother bear, and she was pregnant. I could tell, 'cause when I woke up, my hand was on her belly and I felt the babies moving, I think that was what finally woke me up. Of course I didn't figure that out in the cave, only later when I had time to think. Well, I scooted right out of there before she woke up and ate me. I was really, really, lucky, girls—that's not something you would usually get away with. That spring, when me and another man were hunting, we came across the mama bear with her two cubs. At first she acted like she was going to attack, then she stopped and sniffed at the air— she moved up close and really smelled me over. I guess my smell had become familiar to her while she was asleep and she associated it with something not dangerous to her and her babies, so she shook her head and walked away instead of attacking. I mentioned to my friend that this was the bear I slept with, and wasn't she a beauty."

Adrian shifted his position and waited for the girls to demand more. When one of them started to say something Adrian continued. "So he spread the story, just out of fun you understand, that I had slept with a grizzly bear and fathered her cubs. The story spread like wildfire and has been ahead of me everywhere I go. It's a bit embarrassing, to tell you the truth, but I can't do anything about it. So, now you know—I don't have bear-cub babies, just a wolf and a horse."

When the giggling-laughter settled down again Adrian told Race to get the girls in bed "They've had a long night and a long day, they'll have half a day tomorrow then the training begins. They need their sleep tonight."

CHAPTER 8

ADRIAN AND THE GIRLS REMAINED at the camp site for over two months.

He had intended for them to keep moving, but once he started training the girls, Adrian realized that he needed to devote his full attention to that effort. They were quick learners, but they had to be taught everything from the very beginning. They were too young to have any experience that could be built on.

He began by matching each of them up with a rifle they could handle. He was fortunate that several of the available guns were lightweight, twenty-two caliber rifles—easy to carry, and with no recoil, they were ideal for the smaller girls. The ammo was generally available, which made them popular for hunting small game; but in the hands of a good shot, even a twenty-two was a deadly weapon.

When each girl had her own rifle, he taught them all how to maintain them—take them apart, clean them, and put them back together again. During all this time, he was teaching, mostly by example, gun safety. He told them the rules over and over, corrected them when they erred, and then did it all over again. He obsessively drilled them on gun safety, stressing it to the point that the girls were ready to scream. He made it so repetitious that some of the girls were reciting the rules in their sleep. Adrian turned gun safety into a religion among the girls; he built it into every single lesson, whenever guns were involved.

Good thing about teaching children, they don't have to unlearn as many bad habits and their young minds absorb readily.

When the girls had become used to carrying their rifles everywhere they went, treating them safely, and cleaning them every night, only then did he begin teaching them to shoot. He took them through all the basics of shooting, the various positions, and which positions were best for each situation. He taught them how to control their breathing, how to relax the major muscle groups and to rely on the skeletal bones to support the rifle, not muscles. He taught them how to aim, how to pick out specific small target points to aim at, and what a proper sight picture looked like. Then he taught them how to gently squeeze the trigger until the firing pin dropped. Up to this point they had been training without ammunition—except for some of the older girls when on guard duty, girls who had proven they already knew how to shoot, and how to act safely.

Before the girls got to the part where they actually shot live ammunition Adrian was confident in their ability to act appropriately—and he was proven right, they were flawless in their safety. They also quickly learned to place their bullets on target. Two of the girls he discovered were nearsighted. There were no glasses, so he changed their rifles out for pistols and taught them to shoot at the limits of their vision.

When they were all proficient he gathered them together and said, "You've all done very well, and are great target-shooters, but being a good shot goes to hell when someone is shooting back. Your heart races, adrenaline surges and your fine motor skills go out the window. So I'm going to teach you to shoot under stress. Be advised, this will not be pleasant."

Adrian then set Race up to shoot at a target. "No matter what happens, you are to remain focused on shooting. Control your breathing, make sure of your sight picture, align the sights, and gently squeeze the trigger...just like you've been taught. Ready? Go ahead and start shooting and keep your focus."

Race got into the prone position, and just as she started squeezing the trigger Adrian began slapping her on the butt with a piece of brush and screaming at the top of his voice. Race was so startled that she jerked the trigger, completely missing the target and turned her head to look at Adrian in surprise. Adrian shouted at her "Keep shooting! Don't look away from the enemy, don't look at me! Keep shooting."

When Race had emptied her rifle she had hit the target only once, and that marginally.

Adrian told the other girls, "That's what happens under stress," Adrian said, both to Race and the other girls who were all gathered around. "That's what happens when you're being shot at. Race always hits the bull's eye at this distance. Under stress her shooting went to shit. Now we'll do it again, and again, and again until she learns to hit the target while under stress. Then each of you will do the same. Understand?"

It took a long time for all of the girls to learn the lesson, but learn it they did. Eventually.

During this time, Adrian was also teaching them everything he thought they needed to know. He was surprised at not only how fast they caught on to basic routines and drills, but how much they enjoyed them. The girls loved doing things in unison, and would march in close order drill at the drop of a hat, singing the heavily edited versions of the marching songs he'd taught them. Even during rest periods, one of the girls would call cadence and the other girls would fall into step.

He taught them when and how to take cover—how to choose good spots for taking cover and position themselves for best concealment. He taught them how to spread out when moving across country, how to set up ambushes, making simple booby-traps and hiding them so they wouldn't be seen until too late, and the best way to get out of an ambush. He taught them to infiltrate and to attack and fade-out guerilla style. The girls went on daily patrols of the surrounding area, with Adrian constantly drilling them on every aspect of their training.

In addition to a gun, each girl carried a knife, concealed but accessible, at all times. He taught them basic knife fighting techniques that utilized their youthful speed, and stances that capitalized on their smaller height and weight. Armed with a sharp knife, the girls became extremely deadly in a close-in fight.

Adrian's goal was for the girls to be a well-trained, highly organized, and skilled operating unit by the time they finally got on the road again. They hadn't been tested under fire, and Adrian hoped to hell they never would be—but he knew these girls were not going to be anyone's easy victims again.

Each evening Adrian and Bear went hunting taking two different girls with him, rotating each girl through as often as possible. He taught the girls how to stalk, to use the wind, what to look for, what to listen for. He allowed the girls to shoot the hogs that they found, letting them gain confidence in their shooting ability and seeing the death and destruction they caused firsthand. By the end of the fifth week, each girl had killed a wild hog, gutted, and cooked it. They had also killed and eaten countless squirrels and rabbits with throwing sticks and small spears. He showed them how to make *atlatls*—primitive spear launchers that would give them greater range with their throws—and how to chip stone to create simple but effective blades and arrowheads.

In addition to hunting and self-defense, Adrian taught them everything he could about basic survival. He showed them every edible plant he could find, and described those that weren't in this area, but which would provide valuable vitamins and micro-nutrients to go along with the meat they killed. They learned to build an almost smokeless fire without matches, and what woods to use for cooking, and which to avoid. They learned how to build temporary shelters and how important it was to stay dry and warm. He taught them how to find water and make it safe to drink.

Adrian found that he was enjoying the teaching. He hadn't realized how much he would enjoy it, but he was having a blast, and the girls were eating up the lessons and wanting more as fast as he could deliver. These were things they wanted to learn, knew they could use; lessons that freed them from being dependent on anyone, ever again.

During the time that Adrian was teaching them, they had slowly learned to trust, and then to love Adrian. In a way, he had become a father to them—and grown very fond of them in return, almost as though they were his own daughters. He had become invested in their success at being self-sufficient. It was the best thing he could give them; he knew it, and they knew it.

* * *

The day before they were to go back on the road, Adrian sent the girls on what he called a "Graduation Patrol."

"Ladies," he said to the group assembled in front of him, "this patrol is your graduation. Do everything right, and you will no longer be just a group of girls, you will officially be a patrol unit, each of you a functioning member of that unit. Your assignment is to capture a flag from a designated location on the map. Race will lead the patrol. She will read the map, assign you to your positions and tasks, navigate the terrain and lead you in, get the flag, and lead you out. You are to assume you are in enemy territory from beginning to end, and act accordingly. I'll be watching from various places. This exercise is to show me that you can do all that you need to do without my being present. Any questions?"

The girls, faces and hands blackened with charcoal in a horizontal, tiger-stripe fashion, all shook their heads in silence.

Adrian turned to Race. "Okay Race, take command." Race called the girls into formation, checked their equipment and dress to make sure they were ready to go. She checked that they had their field rations, water, and ammunition. Checked that their guns were cleaned and loaded with one in the chamber, and safeties on. Then she outlined the mission, showed them on the map where they were going, how they would get there and the type of movements they would utilize.

When Race determined they were ready, the unit moved out in two, single-file lines, spaced far enough apart to not make them close together targets, yet still remain in visual contact with each other.

Adrian had placed odd objects along their route to simulate an enemy sighting. Whenever one was spotted by the point person, they gave the signal to drop and cover while the situation was sorted out. Race sent scouts ahead to check the route for terrain problems or enemies, and behind to watch their rear and flanks as they moved slowly and silently, almost invisibly towards their destination.

The girls were absolutely silent, using the terrain to stay as hidden as possible. There was no talking, no whispering. They took this exercise seriously, graduating meant they knew what they were doing and that would please Adrian, failure was just unthinkable. From ten years old to seventeen years old, they treated this with the gravity of adults.

The unit collected the flag and began their return. Per Adrian's instructions they came back by an entirely different route, this one taking them over difficult terrain. It included two stream crossings that required rope work. It also required scaling four steep rock faces to cross two deep ravines. Adrian had pre-warned Race that he had set up an enemy ambush along their return trail. She didn't know where it was or when to expect it because he had only told her to expect it and to treat it as a live fire exercise—the girls would be firing live ammo. This was the most difficult and dangerous training the girls had been exposed to yet, and only Race knew it was coming.

Adrian had made crude dummies of straw and twine. He had chosen the mock ambush location carefully, assembling the straw dummies into a classic ambush from higher terrain.

Adrian watched as the patrol approached the ambush point. He raised his pistol and fired four rounds into the air. This was Race's signal. She looked up where Adrian had fired from and saw the dummies he had set up to resemble the ambush team. Race looked back and saw that the girls had taken cover and had assumed a guns-out position, as they had been trained.

"Ambush, Ambush!" Race yelled. "Take that hill! Advance and cover. Team One, put cover fire onto those enemy soldiers, live rounds, by turns *now!*"

She was almost surprised at herself for automatically giving the correct instructions and by the fact that the girls performed exactly as they had trained to do.

"Team Two, Advance under cover! *now!*"

Again the girls performed flawlessly.

It was, of course, obvious to the girls that this was an exercise, they were after all shooting at dummies. But it was a live fire exercise, shooting real bullets over the heads of their team mates as they advanced, then having live rounds shot over their heads as they leapfrogged past them and took up a forward position. It was exciting and extremely dangerous. One mistake and one of their beloved partners could be killed. The girls focused on what they were doing, and were very careful not to shoot each other. They shot the dummies to pieces, scoring direct hits with almost every shot they took.

It was the work of only a few minutes to over-run the ambushers. The girls leapfrogged up the hill, pouring suppressive fire into the ambush as they covered each other.

When the girls had taken the hill, Race looked around for Adrian but didn't see him. She brought the girls together and had them sit while she critiqued the exercise. "Excellent work team! You followed orders and followed your training almost perfectly. There were one or two minor improvements that could be made, minor but important. Team One, you should not have advanced quite as far as you did each time, you left yourselves exposed to too much fire by trying to cover too much ground. Next time take less ground each time."

She turned to the second group. "Team Two, your rate of fire was a little too fast, slow it down just a hair and you'll be that much more accurate and deadly. Not much, but slow it down just a hair. Okay, let's move out, we've got a couple of hours to go before we get back. Keep your concentration, watch everything, and look for anything that doesn't belong. Rita, you take point. Move out!"

Adrian watched and listened from his hiding spot. He approved of everything the girls had done and the weaknesses that Race had identified. *She is definitely officer material.* When the girls were out of sight he headed straight back to camp. They were armed, and had their adrenalin up from the live fire exercise. This was a dangerous two hours, maybe more dangerous than the ambush exercise itself had been. He had listened to make sure that Race had made the girls put their weapons on safe, but it would only take a second for them to lay down a barrage of fire, and Adrian didn't want them to spot him and spook.

He waited at the campsite for them. *They'll be on their own soon. I could literally leave them right here and they would be fine, but they might be even better off in Corpus...maybe. Either way, I can leave them now and have a clear conscience about it.*

They would be back on the road the next day, and the girls would be tested soon after.

Chapter 9

THEIR FIRST DAY BACK ON the road was uneventful. When they camped that evening the girls automatically exited the back of the truck as though they were in enemy territory. The older girls went out first, rifles locked and loaded. They came out fast, ran, and spread out in a fifty-foot circle surrounding the truck, dropping into a prone position weapons at the ready. After waiting long enough to ascertain that they weren't in immediate danger, they jumped back to their feet and searched the surrounding area silently and effectively, making sure that there were no nearby problems. As they left to perform that chore, the middle girls exited the truck and followed a similar procedure, completely surrounding the truck also. When the older girls returned with the all clear, then the middle girls moved outwards, making a perimeter of fifty yards around the truck. The younger girls exited the truck and moved out in a similar fashion as the other girls had—not so much because it was warranted, but as a matter of practice and discipline.

Until Race gave the all-clear signal, all of the girls were on hyper-alert status, weapons loaded, safeties on. When Race satisfied herself that there was no imminent danger, she gave the signal and the majority of the girls returned and began setting up the camp. Four of the girls stayed at the outer perimeter as sentries.

Adrian had done nothing more than observe. *The girls have it down pat. They are a scary bunch. Feral girls actually. They have their weaknesses, aren't close to invincible, but if they stay alert and follow procedure they'll be safer than most people these days. One of their best weapons is surprise; no one is going to look at them and understand their capabilities until it's too late.*

While the girls were setting up camp, four more of the girls left for a combination long range look-around and hunting trip. They would first scout the surrounding area out to a mile in each direction, then if all was clear they would hunt for as long as they could, knowing to be back just before dark. Two girls went north and two went south, moving out to the mile radius, then circling counter-clockwise until they reached the opposite compass point before they commenced hunting.

Adrian had stressed that they should take every opportunity to avoid being surprised. Surprise should be their weapon, not one they ever allowed anyone to use against them.

That evening he worked with some of the younger girls on knife-fighting techniques. They were pretty good already, but could always be better. He showed them how to use their diminutive size to advantage. There were two primary targets these girls could get to if they had the element of surprise on their side. First target was the femoral artery. Adrian drilled them on its location, and the best thrust-and-slash combination to cut that artery. Once the artery was cut the girl was to run, staying out of reach of the assailant until the blood had pumped out of him.

The second target was the genitals. Adrian stressed that this target might or might not disable their opponent, but wasn't usually fatal. This was to be used only if for some reason the femoral artery was blocked and unavailable. He stressed that it was a poor second choice. It was a shock weapon; an assailant that realized his genitals had been damaged might go into shock or might go into an uncontrollable rage instead, so it was best left as the last possible tactic.

By dark the two long-range teams came in with one young feral hog, two rabbits and five squirrels which they would supplement with canned food. The girls understood the value of the canned goods, which could save their lives if hunting wasn't possible, and were also valuable trade goods. They dipped into that supply as rarely as possible, and then they ate the least popular trade foods first.

The girls took turns on night watch, two hours each, as the others slept. Night watch was a permanent routine now, and would be continued even if they ended up living in a nice house in town.

When the first light in the eastern sky was apparent, the night watch woke up that morning's cooks. This was another group chore rotated among the girls. Those on breakfast duty would stoke up the fires and prepare the morning meal while the others got up, put their sleeping gear in the truck, took care of their morning nature calls, and washed up. As soon as the meal was finished the girls got to work cleaning up the dishes. Cleanup was performed by everyone who was not on an assigned duty at the time. The perimeter guards stayed on guard, their meal brought to them. Their dishes were collected and cleaned. They wouldn't leave their posts until relieved or called in by Race. Without being in a rush, the now well-organized girls were ready to roll forty minutes after the guards woke the cooks. If they were in a hurry they would skip the meal and be loaded and ready to go in less than two minutes. This was an emergency drill that Adrian had taught them and that Race practiced frequently.

Adrian had also been teaching the older girls how to drive the truck. He began by teaching them the basics of how each component of the truck worked, and then gave them simple problems to diagnose. When he was sure they understood the workings in a basic way, then he taught them the maintenance routines. Checking the fluids, belts, tires. What the dash gauges indicated and what would happen when they showed trouble. Only after they had all of that did he begin teaching them to drive.

The girls were extremely fast at learning most things. They quickly understood the basics of internal combustion engines, and drive trains. They got into the preventive maintenance routine quickly and efficiently. But teaching them the physical skills required to drive the truck was fundamentally different. The girls struggled with it. There were practical reasons for their difficulty. The truck did not have power steering and required a great deal of upper body strength at times, especially driving off road. Their shorter legs made it difficult for them to reach and manipulate the foot pedals. Their shorter heights meant that they had less visibility directly in front of or beside the truck. All of these were unavoidable and Adrian could clearly see their impacts.

Driving on paved roads was considerably easier and that skill was the one most quickly attained. By the third day on the road, Adrian had become a passenger, a nearly silent passenger. He rarely had to tell the girls what to do, mostly he observed and only occasionally made a quiet recommendation.

The next morning Race pulled the immediate evacuation drill and timed the girls at ninety seconds. This was a simple exercise. Each girl went to sleep each night with everything already packed on the truck except for their bedrolls and weapons. When awakened by the evacuate signal, three short quiet whistles, they picked up their bedrolls and weapons and piled into the back of the truck. Each girl had an assigned spot in the truck, with the perimeter girls maintaining weapons ready.

Race gave the girls a thumb's up and told them to dismount and prepare breakfast. The cooking utensils were kept on the truck except when in actual use. As soon as the meals were prepared and eaten the dishes and pans were cleaned and returned to the truck. The girls could get into the truck and be ready to roll usually long before the truck could be fired up and ready to roll. For this reason the night watch kept the wood gas generator burning on low all night in case they needed to make an emergency exit from the area. Adrian was teaching the girls to be alert, aware of their surroundings, and ready to act or react on an instant's notice. *Independence comes with a price; constant vigilance, to paraphrase a quote of our founding fathers.*

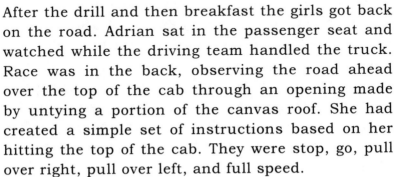

After the drill and then breakfast the girls got back on the road. Adrian sat in the passenger seat and watched while the driving team handled the truck. Race was in the back, observing the road ahead over the top of the cab through an opening made by untying a portion of the canvas roof. She had created a simple set of instructions based on her hitting the top of the cab. They were stop, go, pull over right, pull over left, and full speed.

At mid-morning, they were cruising south on Texas Highway Seventy-Seven, at twenty-five-miles per hour. As they crested a hill they saw four men, armed with rifles, standing beside the road up ahead. The men had obviously heard the truck coming and were waiting to see what it was. As the truck came closer the men moved into the traffic lane, waving their arms for the truck to stop.

Race shouted a warning to the girls in the back, and hit the top of the cab, giving the "full speed" signal. The girl driving pushed the accelerator to the floor. The truck, lumbering downhill, began to pick up speed. This type of truck wasn't known for being fast, and the less-effective wood gas fuel slowed it down even more. Thirty-five was top speed, on level ground. Going downhill it could get up to seventy-miles per hour, but going up a steep hill the truck could slow to as little as ten miles per hour.

The truck sped up as it approached the men and they leapt out of the way at the last moment, two going to each side. As soon as the truck was alongside the men, they opened fire at the tires, scoring several hits. The truck, its tires filled with no-flat foam, kept moving unhindered, but the girls returned fire and the four men were shot down in seconds. Race gave the signal to keep going. She waited until they had gone half a mile, then hit the roof again, giving the signal to "pull over left" into the brush.

When the truck was hidden from the road, Race gave the driver the "stop" signal. Immediately the girls exited the truck as they had been trained, spreading out, creating a secure position. Race then signaled to three of the older girls and left camp to scout where the men had fallen.

CHAPTER 10

ADRIAN WAITED PATIENTLY IN CAMP. At no point, from the moment he had gotten into the truck that morning until after the shooting had stopped, had he given any orders or been asked for any advice. The girls were operating independently of him, and so far had done everything well. *I can leave them with a clear conscience. They don't need me at all. Clearly they can take care of themselves.*

Two hours later the scout patrol came back carrying four extra weapons. Race checked the camp over to make sure everyone was performing their duties, then called a general meeting.

"We found their house—an old farm house a hundred yards off the road. It looks like they'd been there for a month, not much more. My guess is that they were roving around stealing, maybe killing. They didn't have much in the way of food or gear, a real hand-to-mouth bunch. Didn't look like they did any hunting either, lazy. Didn't find any other threats in the area. We pulled their bodies out of sight of the road, took their rifles and ammo. That's all they had worth bringing back. Fairly decent rifles, good trade items. We'll eat a quick lunch then hit the road. Cooks, get the food out."

Race set down next to Adrian.

"I kind of expected to see some of the girls break down and cry after killing people," said Adrian. "Instead they all look as happy as kids on a playground. I'm not sure what to think about that."

"We've had a rough life Adrian," Race said with a shrug. "We were used to believing that we were helpless and we don't much like men after the way we've been treated. Thanks to you and your training, we are getting used to the idea that we aren't helpless. It's a better feeling than I can describe, and we actually proved to ourselves today that we aren't helpless now. The response you're seeing isn't about killing those men, it's about fully realizing and understanding we are independent, a true sense of being able to cope. No one's not exactly happy about killing, but we don't regret it either; we're happy about being able to do what we have to when we have to."

Adrian asked, "So they don't feel any remorse?"

"No, and they shouldn't. We were minding our own business, not harming anyone in any way when those men opened fire on us. Those men shot at us, we defended ourselves. Simple as that, and we were completely in the right. No bad feelings on our side for what those stupid men got themselves into. We didn't ask them to shoot at us, we didn't ask them to attempt to interfere with our liberty. Can you imagine what would have happened if we'd been unarmed and untrained and stopped the truck? Nothing pretty about that, is there? We got it right, and we were in the right. No need to feel bad about anything."

Adrian responded, "Just checking. Looks like the

training is over. You'll need to continue drilling and exercises, that's the way to stay sharp and focused. Every army throughout history has done the same. But my work is done. I know I can move on now, leaving you girls to take care of yourselves, as you have so clearly demonstrated."

Race, with an unusual look of apprehension for her, asked "When?"

"Well, I could go today, but if you're still going to Corpus Christi, then I'd like to hitch a ride that far."

Race said, "Of course you can ride along. We're going to have to settle some place, and once we see Corpus we might decide that it's a good place. Or we might not; won't know 'til we get there." She rubbed her hands together, looked at the girls bustling around camp. "I'm going to have to prepare the girls that you'll be leaving us soon. They've known it of course, but the reality of it hasn't sunk in. I don't want to spring that on them at the last minute."

Adrian asked, "Why's that?"

Race looked at Adrian for a long moment, then shook her head. "You just don't have a clue, do you?" She got up and stalked off.

Adrian watched her go. *Did I just make her mad?*

On the fifth day of travel they came to the small town of Woodsboro, Texas. It was one of several towns they had to drive through because there was no alternate route around them. Driving a truck had several positive benefits, but it also had some negatives—not being able to skip around small towns was a definite negative. The girls were on full alert as they moved through the town as quickly as they could.

In the center of town Adrian spotted a handmade sign that said "Trading Post" over the doors of what had been a local store.

"Pull the truck up in front of that trading post." Adrian told the driver.

She looked at Adrian as though she might not be supposed to taking his orders, but shrugged and complied.

Race was out of the truck before Adrian. She looked furious. "Why did you stop? This isn't a secure location!"

"It's okay Race," Adrian said, smiling at her consternation. "The girls are set to go off like a bomb; and frankly, I am more concerned for the safety of this town's citizens than I am for the girls' safety. Go ahead and keep them on alert, but tell them to put their weapons on safe, and keep their fingers *off* the triggers. I want to see what kind of trade we might be able to do here."

As Adrian finished talking, a man came out of the store; he was unarmed and appeared to be friendly. "Howdy folks! Always a pleasure to meet people traveling through. You all headed for Corpus, I expect."

"How do you know where we're going?" Race asked suspiciously

The storekeeper replied, "Just guessing. There's not much else down this highway, so it kind of figures, you know? You all in a trading mood? I've got some pretty good stuff. Oh, by the way, you're being covered from several places by some really good shots. No offense, but we don't trust just anyone that comes down the road."

Adrian smiled and nodded, "I expected we were, and I expect we will be inside the store, too. That's okay, that's what I would do too. But, just so you know, we're well-heeled ourselves, if anyone around here gets to feeling froggy. I won't go into details, but I can assure you this is one hornet's nest you don't want to kick over."

The storekeeper smiled back, "Now that's alright son, that's alright. It's just good policy on both our parts, eh? Come on in and see what we got. Might find something you can't live without."

Adrian went through the door first. Race waited outside a full ten seconds before she entered. If Adrian has spotted a trap, or didn't like the looks of what he saw, he would have warned her off. Since he didn't she entered.

The inside of the store was set up with warehouse racks. They didn't look natural in the setting, but they were full of stuff. This trading post had a lot of valuable items, items that any raiders would love to have. After looking around for a couple of minutes Race understood that there was a lot here to protect. The storekeeper's assurance that he was protected seemed more realistic once she understood what a rich target this place would be.

The storekeeper asked Adrian, "Is there anything in particular you're short of? I've got something of just about everything."

Adrian shook his head no in reply.

The storekeeper said, "Well just look around to your heart's content. If you see anything you like, make me an offer and we'll see how it goes."

Race spotted coffee. She had never had any herself, but she had heard Adrian once mention how he missed it in the morning. "I've got some canned goods that I'd trade for a tin of coffee."

Adrian looked at her in surprise. He knew she would only be getting it for him, and he was touched. "Race, that's a nice thought, but pretty wasteful. You'd trade calories for my pleasure and I can't have that."

"I didn't ask you, Adrian," Race replied, then quickly continued. "I'm sorry if that was rude; it wasn't meant to be. It's just that you've done so much for us, and we've done nothing in return. I'd like to at least have the pleasure of seeing you enjoy a morning cup of coffee. Please don't interfere, this is my doing."

Race turned back to the storekeeper who had remained silent during this exchange, and raised her eyebrows.

He said, "I'll trade anything I have for anything I think is a good deal for me. Canned goods are always welcome, but for coffee they have to be special canned goods. What do you have worth mentioning?"

"I've got something very rare; rare as your coffee," Race said. "Something that people loved even before the gird went down, and love even more now. I have Spam."

The storekeeper's face immediately showed a sharp interest. "Spam? Oh my, Spam is certainly an interesting commodity. I'll trade coffee for Spam, but not at a one-to-one ratio. Spam is good, no getting around that, but not as good as coffee. I'd trade this two pound can of coffee for, say, ten cans of spam."

Race replied, "Mister I got off that truck, I didn't fall off of it. I'll trade you two cans of spam for two pounds of coffee."

The storekeeper laughed, "Well Miss, I guess you didn't fall off that truck. But that don't mean I'm going to fall on my head either." With a smile he continued, "Why don't we sit down over there and have a cold soda pop while we deliberate. I'm in no particular hurry if you aren't."

They sat down and returned to haggling. Adrian looked over the contents of the shop, then asked Race to step outside with him for a minute. When she complied he mentioned some other items they could use and what he thought they had to trade that would be of interest. He left it up to her to decide if she wanted the items and how much she would trade away for them.

The girls had been allowed to get out of the truck and move around a little. They had naturally taken up a defensive posture. The storekeeper had noticed this and asked Race about it. Race gave him the cover story they'd all agreed on: they had been in an orphanage for girls that had caught on fire and killed the two grownups that ran the institute; Adrian had come along the next day, taken pity on the girls, and decided to help them relocate.

Two hours later Race and the storekeeper were shaking hands on a combination deal for several items, including the coffee.

"She called you Adrian and you have those scars," said the storekeeper. "I'm guessing that you're Adrian Hunter? Better known as General Bear? Am I right? We hear stories about you all the time on my ham radio."

Adrian acknowledged his identity, and listened patiently to the storekeeper's recounting of the stories he had heard, answering questions for minutes that seemed to him like hours before Race interrupted.

"You have a ham radio here? Do you have a transmitter?"

The storekeeper said, "Sure thing, Miss. It's in the back if you'd like to see it."

Race said, "Maybe in a minute. Can I see you outside Adrian?" Adrian, curious about Race's intentions, and more than happy to escape the store keeper, went outside with her.

"Adrian" She said, "Everyone near a ham radio knows that you're more or less engaged to be married to Colonel Linda Fremont. This trader will broadcast the news that you're traveling with sixteen girls before our tail lights are out of sight. It's big news, he's the first to have it, and he'll jump all over it. When Colonel Fremont hears it over the radio, it won't matter what the details are, she's going to be angry and hurt. There's only one thing you can do—you get on this man's radio and you call Colonel Fremont and you tell her yourself that you're taking sixteen orphan girls that you couldn't abandon on to Corpus Christi with you."

"Why will it help to hear it from me?" Adrian asked.

"Jesus, Adrian, you really don't have a clue do you? You can be so smart about so many things, too. It's a damn shame you can't see the obvious— but trust me, I have your back on this. Get on his radio, call her and talk about your trip, and mention us girls. Don't make a big production of mentioning it and don't go into any more detail than she asks you about. Play it cool, like this happens every day to every man on earth. She'll love you for telling her. She'll *hate* it if she finds out from anyone but you. But do it now. If you don't tell her in the next five minutes, she'll hear about it by tomorrow morning from someone who will get pleasure out of being the first to pass on the juicy gossip. And you need to tell her the girls are calling themselves Adrian's Angels."

"Do you really call yourselves that?"

"Not before now, no. But this is important. If we don't name ourselves, the rest of the world will make up a name for us and it might not be a good one. I can think of several names we don't want to be called that could become common."

"What difference does it make? Who cares what they call you?"

"Oh, Adrian, you can be so dense! It makes all the difference in the world. You wouldn't want folks calling us Hunter's Whores would you? Or Hunter's Harem? Or Adrian's Amazons? It's important to us, and if we don't name ourselves, someone else will and we'll have no control over what they come up with. Tell her how well-trained and deadly we are, too, how quickly and thoroughly we killed those men that attacked us...that kind of reputation might help us out some day. Go. Call her. Now."

Adrian made the radio connection to Fort Brazos and Linda was quickly summoned to the radio. He told her about his trip, including a very brief account of finding of the girls—Adrian's Angels—and how he came to be their temporary guardian. She told him of the local news back home. They professed their continuing love, and all-too-soon the conversation was over—and heard by a thousand ham operators all over the world who eagerly passed the news on to everyone around them.

Later, while they were getting the camp settled for the night Race said, "I don't know how to explain it to you, Adrian—either you already understand or you'll probably never understand, so stop asking me. The best I can explain it is this: she'll want to say 'I know' to anyone that comes up to her to tell her about you and all those girls. There's satisfaction in her hearing about it from you directly. Just trust me on this and always remember it. Tell her any news *first*, always, and you're likely to be able to stay together a little longer than otherwise."

CHAPTER 11

THAT NIGHT THE GIRLS MADE a large pot of pinto beans and pork. As Little Faye, one of the youngest girls, took a bowl and went to the bean pot, Lena spotted her and yelled "*No!*"

"Why did you yell at her?" Adrian asked Lena. "Why shouldn't she have beans like everyone else?"

"Because she releases poison gas when she eats beans, that's why," said Lena.

"Oh for God's sake, you have to be kidding me. That little girl couldn't hold a teaspoon of gas. Faye you go ahead and eat the same as everyone else." He addressed the rest of the girls who had started to pay attention. "This is a unit, a tight knit group. You can't single one person out for special treatment if she hasn't done anything wrong. It's just not right to make her watch you eat well while she has to settle for less."

Race had been watching and listening, smiling a bit. "It's her turn to ride in the cab tomorrow, you know."

"It is not, why are you changing the rotation?"

"I determine the roster and make changes as I see fit, and tomorrow she rides in the cab."

"Fine. That's just fine with me. Faye, you eat all the beans you want."

Adrian fell asleep that night thinking maybe he ought to have listened to the girls about Faye. *How bad can that little girl's stomach be? Oh hell, she's just a little kid and I've been around many a grown man with bad gas, no problem.*

Two hours after leaving the camp the next morning, Adrian was sitting in the passenger seat and watching the countryside slide by outside the window when he suddenly let out a yell. "Jesus Christ! Faye! Oh my lord." He frantically rolled the window down and stuck his head out. When the girls in the back saw him stick his head out they began laughing with hilarity.

Adrian spent the rest of the morning with his head mostly out the window and cursing violently. Faye smiled at him frequently. He soon learned that whenever she smiled at him, a gas bomb was about to explode. "Holy shit, Faye! You should've warned me yourself. Is this any way to treat a friend?"

Faye just shrugged innocently, then a little smile came on her face. Adrian quickly stuck his head out the window again. Every time he did, he could hear the girls in the back hooting and laughing.

Adrian called for an early rest stop. "Race, you take Faye into the bushes and don't come back until she's done her business. Damn. Even Bear is suffering."

They traveled for three more days before reaching the outskirts of Corpus Christi in the evening. Faye wasn't allowed to eat beans for the rest of the trip. As they came near the city Adrian called a halt for the day, he didn't want to arrive in the dark. With the first signs of daylight they resumed the last part of their trip.

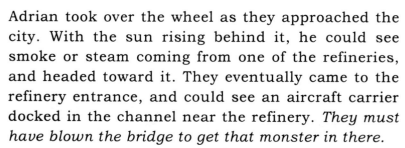

Adrian took over the wheel as they approached the city. With the sun rising behind it, he could see smoke or steam coming from one of the refineries, and headed toward it. They eventually came to the refinery entrance, and could see an aircraft carrier docked in the channel near the refinery. *They must have blown the bridge to get that monster in there.*

At the gate, they were stopped by men in uniform holding their hands up for them to stop. As he slowed to a stop, Adrian shouted out the window to the girls, "Stay in the truck."

He slowly opened the cab door and stepped out, keeping his hands in sight of the guards. They looked nervous. "Hello. I'd like to see your CO."

Recognizing him, the guard laughed and replied, "You already have an appointment. You'd be Adrian Hunter, I presume?"

"How in hell did you know that?" asked Adrian, somewhat startled.

"Just about everyone in Texas knows you're coming to Corpus with a truckload of girls. Who else could you be?"

"Yes, I'm Adrian. What do you mean, I already have an appointment?"

"The Admiral put out the word to let him know if and when you arrive." Pointing to a parking area just inside the gate, he continued, "Park over there and we'll arrange transport to the ship for you."

"What about the girls? I don't want to just leave them here waiting."

"No problem, we've got a bus can take you all on board the ship. I'll call it in; it'll be here shortly. Tell

LLOYD TACKITT

the girls it's ok to get out and stretch, but to leave their weapons on the truck. No offense, but you'll all have to be unarmed to get on the ship."

"And my wolf?" Adrian asked.

"No problem sir, as long as he stays with you at all times; The Admiral has already cleared him."

Adrian knew from his military days that this was lenient treatment and didn't argue. "Understood." He wheeled the truck through the gate and parked it where the guard had indicated. Getting back out of the cab he told Race "Tell the girls to secure arms and come on out and stretch their legs."

As the girls were disembarking from the truck, Adrian looked around at his surroundings. He could see men working in the distance in the refinery. Huge pipes ran everywhere with large tall towers jutting up into the sky at seemingly random locations. Knowing something of the basics of refining from discussions with Matt, he could more or less piece together what he was seeing. In rudimentary terms crude oil was pumped into the refinery where it was heated in a large vessel with a tower on it. As the oil was heated specific elements of the oil were 'cooked off' as the oil reached their specific boiling points. "It's a lot like distilling whisky." Matt had said. "The oil will reach a high temperature then the most volatile stuff will boil off as a chemical steam. When it reaches a certain height in the tower it will be drawn off and condensed back into a liquid state. Except for the certain gasses that will remain in gaseous form. The lighter elements, such as gasoline will come off, then as they're cooked out of the main vessel the temperature will rise again and the next most volatile material will cook off, and so on. This is how they separate gasoline from diesel from kerosene from natural gas. Eventually what will be left in the vessel is a thick tarry substance. Due to the high temperature this can then be pumped out because it will be liquefied and thinned by the heat. After it's pumped away a fresh batch of crude oil will be pumped in and the process starts over again. That in a nutshell is more or less how it works."

The huge aircraft carrier loomed over everything. Men in navy uniforms moved about on deck in a purposeful manner. Even when a ship like this was sitting still, there were, Adrian knew, thousands of tasks that had to be continually carried out. Adrian saw several very large black cables running from the ship and into the refinery area. These he assumed were power cables, transferring electricity from the ship's nuclear reactor-fueled generators to the refinery.

The guard had placed another man in charge of the gate and walked over to Adrian. "It's a real pleasure to meet you sir." He saluted, startling Adrian a bit, but he saluted back automatically. The young guard stuck his hand out and said, "Ensign Fredericks, at your service sir! The admiral has requested the pleasure of your company aboard the ship and asked me to act as your escort."

Adrian shook hands, admiring the young man's crisp clean uniform and military looks. He hadn't seen a man with a short haircut and closely shaved face in a long time, or a man with the obvious pride of military bearing this man had. It was beyond refreshing, it was like a homecoming.

"The shift transfer bus will be here momentarily; while we're waiting, I need to make sure everyone is unarmed. I don't mind patting you down sir, but I'll be damned if I know how to assure the Angels aren't armed. Any suggestions?"

"Angels?" Adrian asked with a bewildered tone.

"Adrian's Angels, sir. The girls. Everyone knows about them."

"Oh, that's right." Adrian said, recalling the name the girls had chosen for themselves. "No, I can't think of anything right off." Turning his head to where the girls were standing, looking at the ship in awe, he called out, "Race, over here, please."

When Race approached, Adrian said, "Race, this is Ensign Fredericks. Ensign Fredericks, this is Race Miller, she's in command of the Angels." He emphasized the word Angels.

Ensign Fredericks shook hands with Race. "Pleasure to meet you ma'am, a real pleasure. I've heard about the Angels and their run-in with the bad guys. Well done, ma'am."

She said, "Thank you, Mr. Fredericks. It is okay to call you 'mister' since you're an Ensign, isn't it?"

"Yes, ma'am, it is. I'm surprised that you know Navy protocol so well. We have a slight problem, we're trying to figure out and maybe you can help. No one is allowed to board ship while armed, except some Navy personnel on official duty. I can pat General Hunter down, but I don't think it appropriate for me to pat down the girls. Have you any suggestions?"

Race turned to Adrian with a questioning look. Adrian replied to her unstated question, "The Ensign is correct, Race. We can't board until he is assured that we are carrying no weapons or other contraband onto the ship."

Race thought for a minute and said, "Do you have a woman on the ship that can perform the search?"

The Ensign slapped his forehead, "Of course," and immediately jogged off to the gate. They could see him speaking into a microphone. After he was finished he walked back over. "I caught them just before the bus was leaving; a female officer will be assigned to ride out here on it and do the pat down. While we wait, are there any questions I can answer?"

Race said, "What's the ship doing here, and what are those cables running from the ship?"

"What we're doing here is a longer story than I have time to tell you right now. But basically those cables deliver electricity from the ship to the refinery. We're making fuel, mostly diesel. We've reconditioned several fishing trawlers to bring in food. The trawlers run on diesel, so it's a necessary step in being able to feed ourselves. We're all a little tired of sea food, but it's all that we have."

"Where are you from, Mister Fredericks?"

"Please call me Eric. I'm originally from Connecticut. My father was career Navy and we moved and lived all over the world when I was growing up. I joined and have been traveling ever since. I've been in the Navy all my life so to speak. We've been docked here for eighteen months now, about the longest I've lived anywhere to tell the truth. How about you Race? Where are you from?"

Before Race could answer an old school bus pulled up to the gate.

CHAPTER 12

RACE TOOK THE GIRLS TO the far side of the bus, followed by the female officer, a Lieutenant—equivalent to an Army Captain. The pat down would take place out of sight of the men in the area. She had a friendly demeanor towards the girls and they didn't seem to be intimidated.

Eventually Race and the female officer, followed by the girls, came out from behind the bus. The Lieutenant approached Adrian and Eric, shaking her head a bit, "Every single one of those girls had a concealed knife on them. Even the youngest. From the way they talked, they have a solid understanding of how to use them, too; they say you've been training them every day." She handed a bag of knives to Eric.

Adrian said, "That's right, I have. Believe me when I tell you they definitely *do* know how to use them effectively."

"Isn't that a bit extreme?" Eric asked. The Lieutenant nodded in agreement with the question.

"Not a bit." Adrian replied. "If you knew the full history of these girls, what they've been up against and what they may come up against in the future, you'd probably agree with me. But agree or disagree, it's the right thing for them to know. It's the right thing for them to have that skill and that tool. I am as pleased as I can be that they have the knives and the skill to use them."

The female officer stuck her hand out to shake. "I'm Lieutenant Jenkins," she said.

"Pleased to meet you Lieutenant." Adrian replied while shaking hands. "We've come a long way to get here, is there any chance these ladies can get a shower and clean their clothes on the ship? Maybe get a health exam by the ship's doctor while we're here? Also I need to stable my horse somewhere."

"Absolutely. I'll see to the girls myself and make sure your horse is properly tended to. Let's board the bus; the Admiral seems impatient to meet you."

Adrian turned to Eric, "Can I see you for a moment in private first?"

Behind the bus, Adrian removed his own knife and handed it to Eric. "Put this in the bag. You forgot to pat me down, and I don't want the Captain to know you missed it."

Eric took the knife with obvious signs of embarrassment. "Thank you sir. That would have been a mark against me." He placed it in the bag of knives he was carrying and they got on the bus. The girls followed quickly.

During this time the girls had been staring at the carrier in awe. The ship was impossibly huge and strikingly beautiful. Old-time mariners were blown away by it, young girls that had never seen any ship before were simply stunned.

The closer they got to the ship the larger it loomed, until when the bus stopped at the dock it became impossible to see its full length and breadth. It blocked most of the sky and seemed to go on forever in all directions.

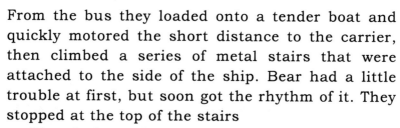

From the bus they loaded onto a tender boat and quickly motored the short distance to the carrier, then climbed a series of metal stairs that were attached to the side of the ship. Bear had a little trouble at first, but soon got the rhythm of it. They stopped at the top of the stairs

"Permission to board?" Eric asked the guard in a formal tone.

The guard replied, just as formally "Permission granted."

As they stepped onto the ship, a long, three-tone whistle rang out. "Admiral On Deck" someone shouted and everyone came to attention; even the girls sensed the requirement of the moment, and stood straighter.

"As you were!" The Admiral said in a normal tone of voice that still seemed to boom around the entire ship's immense inner deck. Everyone returned to their duties immediately, albeit doing those duties a bit sharper than before. The Admiral was a trim man in his sixties with gray hair cut short. He was six feet tall and moved with barely contained energy.

"Mr. Hunter! I've been waiting to see you ever since I heard you were coming to visit! Ladies!" he said, bowing to the group of girls with a smile, "I've been on tenterhooks waiting to meet you as well. We have prepared a late breakfast for all of you in the Officer's Dining Room, please, follow me."

Without waiting for a reply, he turned smartly and led the way. If the ship had seemed huge before, it seemed even larger as they walked past several F-16 fighter jets, then wound their way up and down stairs and in and out of passageways like a maze. It took ten minutes to reach the dining room, where they found plates laid out and platters of food scattered around the table.

"I'm afraid that all we can offer is sea food. It's good fare, but can become monotonous after a few months." the Admiral said with a smile to the girls. "Please sit where you like and eat as much as you want. Water is all we have to drink, but it's purified and will wash the food down adequately. Come, come, sit down ladies, don't be shy. Lieutenant Jenkins, you'll be in charge of the girls for the time being, sit and eat with us. Ensign you may return to your post now. Thank you for bringing them along so quickly. Now, let's dig in!"

The girls had been eating pork and canned vegetables for years and were happy to eat something different. Adrian agreed with them, the seafood was outstanding, a really great change of pace. When the girls finally started showing signs of getting full, the Admiral said, "Ladies may I borrow Mr. Hunter for a few hours? While he's gone would you like a tour of the ship?"

Adrian replied for the girls, "Admiral, I am sure they would love a tour, but I'm thinking they might enjoy a long hot shower and a chance to wash their clothes even more, if that's okay?"

The Admiral saw the delight on the girls' faces and, smiling broadly, said, "Of course! I should have thought of that first thing."

"After that" Adrian said, "Would it be possible for the ship's doctor to give each of the girls a health exam? I don't think any of them are ill, but they won't get this opportunity often and...well...I just want what's best for them."

"Certainly! Another splendid idea sir. Lieutenant, would you make the arrangements? Then a tour if they so please and let's all meet back here for dinner, 1900 hours, yes?"

"Adrian it is then." the Admiral responded to Adrian's request. They were seated in a pair of comfortable arm chairs in the Admiral's quarters. "Please call me Jim in private, but please do continue with 'Admiral' in front of my crew."

At that moment there was a knock at the door, and a sailor brought in a tray with a thermos of coffee and two cups.

"I apologize for not having sugar or cream, but what little we have is needed for higher purposes. This coffee is a rare treat in itself; we have almost none left and only bring it out on special occasions. This, my friend, is a special occasion. There are damn few heroes that come to visit."

Adrian started to protest, but was quickly cut off.

"Hero you are sir, most definitely," insisted the Admiral. "The entire country is talking about your exploits and if they are only half true you are still a most singular hero and apparently a modest one to boot. Even if I hadn't thought so before, your rescue of those young ladies would put you firmly in that category without assistance. Please, tell me their background, their story."

Adrian started at the beginning, then filled in details of their journey and training. The Admiral asked only a few questions, nodding often, smiling once or twice, frowning only when Adrian described how Race had killed the trader they got the truck from.

Adrian concluded, "Admiral, those girls were forced into prostitution. It would be better for them if that was kept silent. If they want to tell anyone about it, that's up to them. I'm requesting your confidentiality on that."

"No need to have asked, that's a given." The Admiral replied. "What an amazing story. Now, I'm intrigued to know what your future plans are for them?"

Adrian grew visibly uncomfortable at the question. "That's the rub, sir. I have to leave them here in Corpus Christi for a few weeks, maybe even a few months. I'm going on a scout into south Texas, then up to San Antonio and Austin. After that I'll swing back and check on the girls, and if they want I'll take them back to Fort Brazos. I hate to leave them, but I can't take them on a long journey like that, not knowing what's out there or how bad it might get."

The Admiral took a sip of coffee, then putting down his empty cup said, "That's pretty much what I thought you'd say and I approve. As a matter of fact it fits in neatly with plans of my own, plans that I hope to include you in. I'll make it a special project of the Navy to oversee the girls' safety and health while you're gone."

"Plan sir?" Adrian wasn't comfortable using the Admiral's first name, no matter how sincere the request. *This is a man in charge of thousands, a bona-fide member of the United States military. He commands a huge aircraft carrier and is no doubt fleet commander of many more ships as well. First name doesn't feel right.* "What plan would that be Admiral?"

"I'll have to give you some background so you'll understand. Navy ships are built to withstand EMP blasts. They're hardened against it, so much of the Navy's fleet was intact and operational after the solar storm. All of our battle fleet of ships are nuclear fueled so we weren't adrift. Nevertheless, after the solar storm, we eventually lost communications with the political authorities. The military as you know is commanded by the President of the United States. We could talk to him for a few months, but then we lost contact with him as well."

"Our first major response was to sail to our foreign ports and pick up as many overseas military men and women and their families as we could, and bring them on board. This was a difficult undertaking with our limited communications and took us nearly two years to complete. We picked up about fifty-percent of the troops out there. I hate that we couldn't get them all, but we couldn't. Once we completed that mission then we had to consider what to do next. With no orders coming from the President we convened a council, by encrypted radio, and determined our next move. This is confidential information by the way, not to be shared with anyone."

"Of course," replied Adrian.

The Admiral continued. "After several weeks of deliberation, we decided to split the nuclear carrier force, sending each carrier and a contingent of nuclear submarines to a separate U.S. port refinery, along with an equal distribution of all other operational

LLOYD TACKITT

ships. My group came here. Our plan, such as it is, is to fire up the refineries and make fuel. We need fuel for our own purposes—even nuclear fuel rods will only last so long without replacements, and many Navy ships are diesel-fueled, as are most fishing trawlers. We are hoping that soon we can make surplus fuel to be distributed to the civilian world to help them restart civilization."

"You must realize that each passing year our ships degrade and need maintenance, but maintenance at the level we need is no longer available. We can keep going for a few more years, but eventually each ship will reach a point of inoperability and have to be abandoned. Civilization and industry need to be restarted and fast."

Adrian nodded in silence, sipping at his coffee as the Admiral continued.

"Getting crude oil is the biggest challenge at the moment. We're drawing crude from the U.S. oil reserves, but that will be depleted within a year. We're also in the process of restarting off-shore oil platforms and getting that crude to the refineries. It's a challenge we can handle though, and within a few more months supply will no longer be an issue. We'll have surplus crude and might then be able to start up other refineries. With enough fuel to bootstrap us up, we can generate electricity conventionally and carry on with the refineries."

Adrian interrupted with a question. "What's the long-term plan for the Navy if the original U.S. government doesn't start up again—and I don't see how it can."

"Well now, that's a damn good question and

the chief question we're still coming to terms with. We've ruled out starting a government ourselves. Our naval historians tell us that a military-formed government will eventually become a dictatorship. Eventually they always turn into tyrannies of one kind or another. We don't want that. Currently our thinking is that we will maintain security for the nation as best we can, provide what support we can, and hope that a strong civil government emerges from the ashes. If that government is one based on personal liberty, then we will subsume to their authority. Until then, there isn't much we can do except make fuel and catch fish."

"Our ability to protect our former nation is limited. A developing security threat may be on the horizon, but it will come by land, probably from Mexico. And that's where you come in, if you choose to."

CHAPTER 13

"I'M ALL EARS ADMIRAL."

"We have limited intelligence capabilities Adrian. Our aircraft are mostly nonoperational. These are delicate machines that take constant maintenance and repair. We're no longer receiving replacement parts, and have to cannibalize parts from other aircraft to repair those few we still have flying. They aren't much use for gathering intelligence anyway, they can't see much in the way of gathering threats. What we do have is radio. We listen to everything that is being broadcast everywhere. We've been picking up little bits and pieces of radio traffic from deep in Mexico. We're interpreting this incomplete information and we think, and I stress *think*, that there is a movement gaining ground to invade Texas."

"The Mexican government is in good enough shape that they can do that?" Adrian asked somewhat shocked.

"No Adrian, not the government—it cratered like ours did. Like almost every other government that we're aware of. There are exceptions, China for one. This movement seems to be coming from the former drug cartels. It makes a strange kind of sense. They were large and well organized. Well-armed and completely ruthless. Even the Mexican government was in fear of them. But now there is no drug trade. They either have to find another *raison d'etre* or they dissolve, completely ceasing to exist. The question is one of motivation, what motivated the drug lords to become drug lords in the first place. The answer is simple once you boil it down: power. They want power. It appears that they intend to regain their power by invading and taking over the United States, starting with Texas."

"That seems to be a mighty big undertaking." Adrian responded.

"Yes, well it is, but it is also quite possible. With enough manpower they can pull it off because there is no central authority that can rally enough troops to stop them. They'll move north through Mexico, gaining men as they go—thousands of men. They'll loot and pillage their way north, and continue until they get so far into Canada that there's no place else to go. They'll pick up more men here in the States too. Their success will cause perhaps hundreds of thousands of Mexican men to flow up behind them. They'll leave presidios behind to maintain control, impose high taxes, and treat everyone as serfs. It's bold, it's ambitious, and it's also, unfortunately, doable."

"Our best bet is to wait until they begin to coalesce and move north, then our aircraft have a chance—a slim chance but a chance—to break their backs. If we can break their morale before they get here we might avert a huge catastrophe. Maybe. If it gets down to the really dirty necessity of it, we still have some tactical nuclear weapons. I'm hoping, no,

I'm actually *praying*, that it doesn't come to that. No long-lasting good can come of that."

"All I can say is Wow. That's a hell of a lot to take in. Where do I fit into this?" Adrian asked gravely.

"Now you see why I took the time to give you the background," said the Admiral. "What we need is on-the-ground intelligence. We need to know what's happening, and where, and when. We can't get that by sitting here listening to infrequent radio traffic. We need men out there who are watching and listening. We need men down in Mexico who can report to us."

Adrian opened his mouth, but the Admiral held up his hand. "Before you say anything, let me tell you I *don't* want you going into Mexico, for a lot of solid reasons. What I *do* want you to do is to report to me on a regular basis what you're hearing *near* the border. I want you to recruit Mexican-Americans to travel down into Mexico, join the cartels themselves if possible, and report back. In effect, I want you to do some low-level spying and some high-level spy recruiting."

"I speak fairly decent Spanish and I can recruit an interpreter, so why not go into Mexico myself?"

"You're a celebrity, you'll be spotted immediately. You'll be as welcome as a roach on a wedding cake, and stand out even worse. Your scars are too visible and everyone, and I do mean everyone, knows about them. There is no reason to believe that anyone down there would tell you anything useful anyway—not a *gringo*, not any *gringo*."

"I can see your point. But you're not really asking a lot of me."

"It may not seem like a lot to you, but it's a critical mission, extremely critical, and you're uniquely qualified for the job. You're famous, you'll be welcomed everywhere you go *in Texas*. Everyone already knows you're going down there to look around, so suspicion will be minimal. Your unique fame will make it far easier for you to inspire men to go down and live on a knife's edge of death. They'll know what will happen if they're caught, and not many men will be likely to take that risk if just anyone asks them. I believe that you will be able to send more men down faster than if I sent out a party of one-hundred individuals to recruit. Your coming here at this time is a Godsend, almost a miracle. The timing couldn't have been better and a better recruiter probably doesn't exist."

"That's laying it on a bit thick isn't it?" Adrian asked with an embarrassed smile.

"No sir, I'm not. If you could look at yourself objectively, and in a global sort of way, you'd see just how rare an opportunity you are for me. Will you do it Adrian?"

"It could mean a much longer absence from the girls Admiral. Are you willing to give me your word that you will personally see that no harm comes to them before I get back? That's the crux of it for me. I find myself with an unexpected obligation here, and it has become close to my heart. Those are fine girls, and I've grown attached to them. We've become something of a family, and family comes first in this world, especially as it is now."

"Absolutely I will. I give you my word of honor and will swear on a Bible or cut my thumb and you cut yours and we'll be blood brothers. Any way I can prove to you, I'll do it."

Adrian sat silently for a minute, thinking it over. "Admiral, there's one other stipulation that I have to make. You'll probably not like it, but it's a deal breaker if it's not met."

"What's the stipulation?" asked Admiral with a slight frown.

"I have to tell the girls what I'll be doing while I'm gone. They need to know that I'm not staying away from them for so long without a damn good reason. They've known from nearly day one that I intended to go on without them at some point, but as we grew closer I could sense that the separation is going to bother them, maybe a lot. Some of these girls are very young and I am perhaps the first stable and non-threatening influence they've experienced. Leaving, even for the few weeks I had planned on was going to be difficult at best. Leaving for a much longer time, well that could be a real problem if they don't understand the full reasoning behind it."

"Can you guarantee their silence on this?" the Admiral asked.

"Guarantee? No, but I'm damn sure of it. As long as I explain everything thoroughly and swear them to secrecy and assure them I'm coming back for them afterwards...I'm not worried about it."

"It's a deal then. Since I'll be personally watching over them, I can remind them from time to time as well. When were you planning on leaving? I'd like to take several days of your time to be trained by an intelligence team on the details of recruiting and communicating before you go. Also, like you, I have one last request, but it's not a deal breaker: I'd like you to take three of my men with you."

"Without even knowing who you want me to take, three is too many. Two, I think, would be better for this trip. Who are they?"

"Two then. One can do double duty. I want you to take an interpreter that's fluent in Spanish, or rather Mexican, which is something else again. We have several in intelligence that speak the language. The other is our Naval historian."

"Historian? That's out of left field."

"Yes, well it would seem that way at first. But hear me out. He's a fit young man and won't be a hindrance in your travels. He's also extraordinarily intelligent and can bring perspective to situations you wouldn't have otherwise considered. His advice is valuable, and he can radio in much more detailed descriptions of your journey, and the people you talk to and what they said than you can. He's trained to record things as they are, objectively and factually. You'll benefit from his advice and I'll benefit from his detailed reports."

"If you say so Admiral, but I retain the right to send either or both of them back if it becomes a problem."

"Done."

There came a knock at the door. It opened, and Lieutenant Jenkins and another officer were standing in the open doorway. "Permission to enter Admiral?"

"Come in, we were just wrapping up here."

"Admiral, Mister Hunter, we've gotten the girls

bathed, their clothes washed and dried and Bones has given them all a health check. As the doctor was examining the girls, in my presence of course, he discovered something a bit odd. He took the liberty of calling in our psychologist here to chat with the girls. He'd like to make a report."

The Admiral said, "Come in and sit down. Dr. Andrews, go ahead, what do you have?"

Dr. Andrews, the ships psychologist started, "To put it bluntly, all but two four of the girls from the onset of menses have been sexually abused, multiple times. Bones discovered this and called me in to talk to them. I discovered that Adrian rescued the girls from a whore house where they had been held against their will and forced into prostitution. These young ladies are dealing with it pretty well, given the circumstances. They've also formed an extremely strong bond to Mr. Hunter; he's become their surrogate father. This bond is, in large part, perhaps why they are handling the abuse as well as they are. But there's a problem coming up. They know he will be leaving them behind soon, and they are very worried about it—some to the point of being quite distraught. I wanted to warn him, and you sir, of the consequences of that separation. Another large part of their coping ability comes from the training Mr. Hunter provided them. He has given them a strong sense of self-esteem based on their learning to fend for themselves, and the manner in which he has woven them into a strong and positive group. But the separation, that could break all of that down."

There was a long silence. Then the Admiral said "I

know about the forced prostitution, this is a subject that remains entirely confidential, not that I need to say that to any of you. But to reinforce it, I am saying it: This is confidential information. Only the girls, themselves can make that knowledge public, and only if they want to on their own. Frankly, I would discourage them from doing so if they showed any inclination."

"Adrian will be leaving in a few days. We need to get the girls situated in that time and I want you three as a team to come up with a plan on how to minimize their anxiety as much as possible. I'm thinking that we might want to house them aboard ship, what do you think?"

"I think it's a good idea." Adrian interjected. "But let's ask them and see what they think. And I'd like to have final approval on the plan to ease their anxiety."

"Excellent idea. Lieutenant Jenkins, why don't you have the girls gather in the Officer's Mess again. Let's feed them and talk to them. I think Adrian will want to talk to them privately first though, to prepare them."

CHAPTER 14

ADRIAN AND BEAR ENTERED THE Mess, closing the door behind him. The girls were seated at the table that was laden with food. Bear had acted with supreme dignity throughout what Adrian felt must be a trying ordeal for him.

"I've good news and bad news, well...not bad news just some not so good news. First though I have to swear each of you to complete secrecy. What I have to say cannot, I repeat...*cannot* leave this room."

Race replied. "Anything you say Adrian. What's this about?"

"Raise your right hands and place your left hands over your heart." When all had done so, Adrian continued. "Do you solemnly swear that what I'm about to tell you will not be repeated to anyone, anywhere, at any time?"

A subdued chorus of "Yes's" and "I do's" followed.

"Okay then. Here's the top-secret stuff." Adrian explained about the possible Mexican incursion into Texas that the Admiral was worried about. It didn't take long. "Any questions?"

"That's bad Adrian. Really bad. What can be done about it?"

"The Admiral has a plan, and he wants me to play a role in his plan. I'll be going along the border, more or less as I was going to anyway, and recruiting spies to go into Mexico and report back on what they're doing. I won't be going into Mexico myself, the Admiral thinks that would be a mistake."

Looking a little bit relieved Race said, "We're glad you won't be going down there." Then, with a look of foreboding, as though she already knew the answer, she asked, "When do we leave?"

Adrian scowled. "Race, you know damn well I wasn't taking you girls on this leg of the trip. I was planning on leaving you here and eventually coming back for you as I've told you several times. Now... now that I've gotten to know you girls better it's more difficult to leave you, but I still plan to do it."

He looked down at his hands, and couldn't seem to figure out anything to do with them. "Okay the good and the bad. Which do you want first?"

"The bad first." Race replied solemnly.

The bad is that I'll have to be gone longer than I had originally planned.

"How long?" Race quickly interjected, showing a hint of tension.

"I'm not sure exactly. I had planned on moving fairly steadily, making the trip in a few weeks. Now I'll be stopping to recruit spies. Each stop could take a few days. I might be gone a few months instead of a few weeks, I'm not really sure."

"Months?" Three of the girls groaned out with dismay.

"I don't really know but it's best to be prepared for what may be a long time don't you think? That way if I get back sooner it'll be a nice surprise."

"So, what's the good news, if there really is any."

Race mumbled with obvious disappointment at this news.

"The good is that while I'm gone the Admiral has agreed to keep you girls here on the ship, safe and protected and well-fed. You won't have to fend for yourselves. I won't have to worry about you while I'm gone, and you'll have a blast living on ship. Showers and clean clothes and three meals a day. You'll live like Queens."

"Jesus, Adrian!" Race said with anger, her chair falling to the carpet with a dull *thud* as she jumped to her feet. "We'll be fucking prisoners! You taught us to look after ourselves then you put us in a steel-hulled prison!" Tears were flowing steadily while Race stared at Adrian with anger.

"Prison?" Adrian asked in confusion. "I thought it would be a life of luxury and safety! How in the world could you call this a prison? For one thing the ship is huge, you won't be confined to a single room, you know. You'll be able to roam the ship as you please—barring secured areas, of course. Plenty of food and hot water. Most people out there would kill to take your place. What the hell are you talking about?"

"I'm talking about us being confined to this ship, that's what I'm talking about. Okay so it's a big prison, with lots of benefits, but it's still a damn prison." The other girls were nodding their heads in agreement, mostly because they trusted Race's judgment.

Adrian was stunned. He had actually thought the girls would be happy and relieved to be taken care of by the U.S. Navy while he was gone. There was a long silence as everyone thought over what had just been said.

Race, understanding that she had a small window of opportunity, went into negotiation mode.

"Here's the deal Adrian. We'll agree to stay, but on our terms. Otherwise we split and take our chances on our own. We want freedom. We want to be able to leave the ship whenever we want to, and stay gone as long as we like. We want the truck, our guns, and all the food on the truck. We want it parked nearby and ready to go whenever we get the urge. Say no to this and there's no deal." Race crossed her arms and stared stubbornly at Adrian. The other girls chorused in agreement.

Adrian stared back just as stubbornly. He deliberately crossed his arms mimicking her body language. He was well aware that Race had the upper hand, her threat of pulling out was intolerable to him and she knew it. "You have a point I guess. If you're not prisoners then you have to be able to come and go as you wish. I just don't see any point in your leaving such a great set-up, and I'll be a lot easier in my mind knowing your safe." Adrian was going for the emotional appeal.

Race knew she was in the driver's seat too and almost smiled, but she was a better negotiator than that. "We spent a lot of time training and I don't want that to go to waste, we don't want to get rusty," she said, countering his emotional appeal with logic. "We'll need to go out for a few days at a time every couple of weeks to continue drilling and training, to keep that sharp edge you always talked about. We can't live here forever and we need to stay independent."

Damn, she's too good at this. Adrian was stumped. She was right and he knew it, yet he suspected there was more going on here than she was showing. "Okay, two days every two weeks for training, and you have to take an adult along with you." He was bluffing with a bad hand and knew it, and knew that she knew it as well.

Race countered, "Four days every two weeks and no adults. If we're going to be self-sufficient, we can't take a crutch to lean on."

Adrian made his last offer. "Three days every two weeks, you show the Admiral where you'll be on a map, you take a radio and check in every twelve hours with an update and current situation report, no adult—and if you're not back in three days, the Admiral sends out a crew to bring you back in and you don't get to go back out again."

Race made her final offer. Adrian could see in her face that this was going to be the bottom line. "I'll stipulate to that, but we need camouflage uniforms and what I said about keeping the truck and arms and food handy still goes, and we get hand-to-hand combat training from the Marines."

"You agreed to all of that?" said the Admiral. "Have you lost your mind? I'm having second thoughts about you Adrian...can't even handle a group of girl scouts by God."

"Either that or they bail. You have no idea how tough those girls are, and Race...she's a terror at negotiating. You watch, in two weeks or less you'll quit having second thoughts and realize that it was the best deal I was going to get. She'll have you in knots before you know what happened." Adrian said with a big smile. "If you're not careful she'll be running the ship in a month."

"Damn it Adrian, this is a U.S. Navy warship. Playing nursemaid to a bunch of little girls is outside my job description. I'm only agreeing because I need your help and you know it."

"Word of honor Admiral, I didn't intend to be in this situation either, but it's either take them back to Fort Brazos right now and forget about heading south for months, or..."

The admiral, with obvious irritation interrupted. "I get it Adrian. So it shall be."

Adrian spent the next two weeks discussing the upcoming trip with the Admiral, Jose Anterres, the intelligence expert, and Ryan Thomas, the ship's historian. He immediately liked the two men. Jose was multi-lingual, speaking six languages including "Mexican". Ryan was a surprise. Adrian thought the Admiral's logic of having detailed reports was a bit overboard but was willing to go along with it. But Ryan, Adrian soon learned, was far more than a mere recorder of events. They had already gotten into many long discussions about historic events and Ryan's perspective on them was unique. He specialized in what he called "Critical Moments", and how the future could have been radically different so many times in so many ways, depending often on bizarre and seemingly inconsequential events and decisions.

"For instance" Ryan was saying, "The outcome of the Civil War could have been so different many times. The future isn't ordained you know; small, simple things can cause big, radical changes."

"Like what?" Adrian asked.

"A simple example. The first battle of Bull Run, also called the first battle of Manassas, was a resounding Confederate victory. The Confederate troops had the Union troops in a panicked retreat. The south, conceivably, could have won the war at that point by going straight to Washington D.C. and capturing the seat of the Union government. It was within their grasp, but not within their imagination. If the Confederate troops had taken D.C., it's very possible that the war would have ended right there with a negotiated settlement. What would the future have looked like if that had happened?"

Adrian also spent a lot of his time with the girls, making sure they were settled in. The girls had quickly captured the hearts of the ship's crew. They had virtual free rein to roam the ship and charmed everyone they met. Adrian suspected that Race had planned this out. When the girls were outfitted with their camouflage uniforms they were even "cuter" in the crew's eyes. Adrian was skeptical. *They only see the surface, underneath is a scheme of some kind. They're up to something.* But he had to admit, the girls had been on their best behavior. The two weeks were blurring by fast and Adrian was eager to get started.

Before leaving Jose showed Adrian the small but powerful radio sets they were taking along to provide the potential spies. "They are long range, use very little power and have collapsible solar panels for charging the batteries. These little guys have encryption built into them. No one will be able to understand what is being said. They also include a burst recorder."

Jose explained that a burst recorder was a device that allowed the sender to record his message prior to transmitting. The message was converted into a high speed burst that, for a simple message, would take only seconds to transmit. The receiving end would record the burst, slow it down and then the operator would listen to it at normal speed. The advantage of this was to make the radio impossible to triangulate, due to its very short duration of transmission. Given the short duration of the transmission it would also be far less likely for a transmission to even be discovered, denying the enemy knowledge that a radio was in use.

CHAPTER 15

A DRIAN, RYAN AND JOSE PUT their heads together to come up with a mode of transportation for the trip. They considered horses and ruled them out, they had too much to carry without adding a string of pack horses. Ultimately that would be too slow, there was a sense of urgency about this mission. They thought about another truck like the one the girls had, but it was too big for what they wanted. The three of them drove around the city in a jeep looking for a likely suspect.

"That's it!" Jose shouted, pointing at a UPS truck.

Ryan said, "Hell, yeah, that's the ticket. It'll carry everything we need out of sight, and leave room to sleep in if we need to. Those things were universal back in the day, they went everywhere. I bet they kept the maintenance up on them as well as the Navy does, being a fleet and all."

Adrian looked and nodded "Let's see if we can find their fleet headquarters, then we can look through all of the inventory that's still parked and choose the best one. Probably pick up oil and filters and other maintenance supplies in their shop—and any tools and spare parts we might need too."

It didn't take them long to find a phone book in one of the abandoned stores, look up the address and check it on their map. Within two hours they were walking along rows of UPS trucks, dozens of them. First they checked the mileage, looking for the lowest mileage they could find. They were in luck and found one that was nearly new. The tires looked new, too, although dry-rot was beginning to set in, as it was on tires everywhere.

They towed the truck to the vehicle maintenance shed and opened the bay doors for light. They chose one tool box, a large rolling-style that appeared to have every tool imaginable inside. Then they loaded up spare tires, oil, filters, belts, spark plugs, plug wires, and anything else that looked useful. Even with all this gear stored in the built-in shelves in the back, the truck still had room.

They towed the truck back to the ship and asked the Chief Engineer to come see it.

When he arrived Adrian said, "This is the truck we want to use Chief. It will need several modifications, though."

The Chief had been ordered by the Admiral to give the men whatever assistance they needed. "What kind of mods do you want"

Adrian handed the Chief a list of items that the three men had come up with together. It included repainting the truck a light tan color, removing the storage racks in the back, replacing the engine with a multi-fuel engine or modifying the engine it had—whichever would be best, a larger alternator and battery, spotlights on all four corners of the top that could be adjusted from the cab, rifle racks in the front and back, hammock connections for three hammocks, a small cook stove, foam filling for the tires and extra foam to take on the road, and a powered antenna suitable for the radio they would be using.

"And" Adrian said "We need a wood gas generator installed so that we can run the truck on wood gas after we run out of diesel. Wouldn't mind some armor plating around the cab either, if you can swing that."

"All easy enough" The Chief replied, "but that plating is heavy stuff, it'll slow you down and burn fuel—I can do it and will, just want to let you know."

"That's expected Chief. When can we have it for a test run?"

"When do you want it? Admiral said it's priority one."

Two days later Adrian was admiring the truck.

The Chief was pointing out the modifications his crew had made. "First thing we did was change the suspension to support the armor plate. Almost called you to ask if you'd rather start with an armored truck, but they don't have much room in back. Notice we put the wood gas generator up front so you can keep an eye on it while you drive. It's a horizontal generator instead of vertical, but it does the trick; we tested it. Making it horizontal lowered the center of gravity, makes it easier to see over, and let us mount it closer to the engine. Notice that it's armor plated, too."

Adrian inspected the generator, and nodded his approval.

The Chief continued. "We made some modifications to the existing engine so that its multi-fuel. There's a bank of switches under the hood, here..." he raised the hood and pointed to the switches, "These switches change the computer system to account for the different fuels; just switch it to the fuel you're using. It turned out to be easier to do this than to completely re-configure the engine support and drive train system. It's a good engine and will work out just fine."

Walking around to the rear of the truck, the Chief opened the back doors. "Everything you asked for, plus we added armor back here as well. It goes along both sides and the doors, but only halfway up. We put in five gun ports, two on each side and one in one of the back doors. Notice we took off the old doors and made new ones that open out more, and they're armored halfway up too. Tool box is secured in the corner there, spare parts are secured in a steel box, extra tires mounted to the inside roof, out of the way. We included a small compressor should you need one, doesn't take any room at all and might be handy. Hammock mounts so the three of you can sleep in the back if you're good friends. Foamed the tires and there's extra foam in the spare parts box. Take it for a spin, give it a hard test, let me know if we need to change anything."

"Wow!" Ryan said, "every boy's dream, eh?"

The Engineering Chief replied, "Well, had it been me specifying the upgrades I'd have put a revolving turret on the top with a chain gun in it. Mount two recoilless rifles on the side and put a belt fed in the back. But that's just me." The Chief then walked off leaving the three men staring.

Adrian said in awe, "I like how he thinks!"

Jose asked, "Should we get him to do that?"

"No, I don't think so. It would be severe overkill for our mission to be armed like that. But it does give me one hell of an idea. After we spin this baby around a few times I'm going to visit the Admiral."

"The reason I wanted to see you is the Chief gave me an idea Admiral. How difficult would it be to find large, four wheel drive trucks, and rig them out sort of like a swift boat?"

"Say again?" The Admiral asked, obviously puzzled.

"Swift boats on wheels. Take a 4x4 truck and mount chain guns, recoilless rifles, small cannons, whatever on them. Make them rolling barrage platforms. Imagine the effectiveness of these against Mexican ground troops. One of these would be as valuable as a hundred men with rifles. There must be thousands of suitable trucks in Corpus Christi waiting for conversion. You'd only be limited by the amount of arms that you can scrounge up to put on them, and the crew time it would take. When the war comes, if it comes, they'd be worth their weight in coffee." Adrian said with a grin.

The Admiral stared at Adrian. Adrian could see the thought taking hold as the skin around the Admiral's eyes crinkled slightly. "You know, that's a damn good idea. The engineering crew is busy as hell with getting the refinery and oil production running, but still..." His voice trailed off as he gave it more thought. "I'll talk to the Chief about it tonight. We have plenty of unskilled men to find and bring in the trucks, and I'll check with armory to see what our inventory looks like. I wouldn't be surprised if we couldn't make half a dozen or more of them fairly quickly. Given time we might make a lot more. You say the Chief gave you the idea? Good, then he'll probably have some sound ideas already in mind. Yes, I like it, I like it a lot. Our Marine and Seal Teams could put these to good use."

"One more thought Admiral. Could the Chief make modifications to the Angel's truck? Not chain guns of course, but radio and armor and one of those wood gas generators he made for our truck?"

"Of course, no problem. Although, now that I'm getting to know the girls a bit better, I have to say 'Angels' seems a bit on the optimistic side. Those girls are damn near feral, Adrian. I'm not sure they should be trusted out of sight...No, don't get alarmed, a deal is a deal, no matter what second thoughts I'm having."

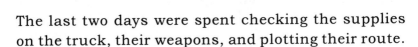

The last two days were spent checking the supplies on the truck, their weapons, and plotting their route.

Adrian, the Admiral, Ryan, and Jose were sitting at the Admiral's table going over a map of Texas. Adrian, tracing the route with his finger tip said, "We'll take Highway 77 to Kingsville, then follow it all the way to Harlingen. In Harlingen we'll switch to Highway 100 and take it to Brownsville. From there we'll get on 281 and follow the border west until we get to Pharr. From Pharr we'll go on to Laredo. From Laredo we'll continue heading west on Farm to Market Road 1417 here, then Farm to Market Road 1021 to Eagle Pass. From there we take 277 to Del

Rio. From Del Rio we cut back to Corpus, crossing south of San Antonio. We'll be covering a lot of miles with frequent stops for intelligence gathering and recruiting. It's rough and desolate country and will have its full share of outlaws. It's a long trip. I'm guessing two months or so, but this route takes us right along the border, where we want to be to get information. Any questions?"

"Can you carry three months' of food for three men?" The Admiral asked.

"We can't. We could carry a month's supply of MRE's if you had them, but you'll need them for the Marines if they get activated. We'll take a week's supply of canned food and water. The rest we'll hunt or scrounge along the way. There's always plenty of rattlesnakes down there. A man can hardly walk twenty feet without finding one, and they're pretty good eating." Adrian was watching Jose and Ryan's faces as he said this, hoping to get a rise out of at least one of them. All he got were two grim smiles.

"Water won't be a big problem, we won't be far away from the Rio Grande once we start moving along the border. It'll be close enough we can make a run to it if needed. We're taking plenty of water purification tablets and micro-filters too."

"Our radio reports will be sent in every day at 1900 hours, the frequency is already set. If we hear something interesting enough, we'll let you know as soon as we can. Otherwise, you'll hear from us every evening."

The Admiral said, "Alright Adrian, sounds like you've got it figured out as well as it can be figured out. I'll say goodbye now, I won't be able to see you off in the morning."

The three men left the Admiral's dining area. They would leave at four in the morning.

Adrian went to say goodbye to the girls.

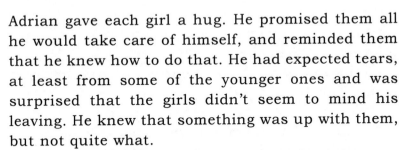

Adrian gave each girl a hug. He promised them all he would take care of himself, and reminded them that he knew how to do that. He had expected tears, at least from some of the younger ones and was surprised that the girls didn't seem to mind his leaving. He knew that something was up with them, but not quite what.

"Race, I want one promise from you. You won't try to follow me. You're up to something and I don't know what it is, but if you're thinking of following me...don't."

"We'll live within the strict confines of our agreement Adrian."

Adrian left satisfied with her response. It wasn't until much later that Adrian thought over her words and realized that she hadn't actually given him a direct response to his demand.

CHAPTER 16

S IX WEEKS LATER THE TRIO had reached Zapata. They were camped outside of town, well off the road. Summer was coming on strong and it had been a hot, dusty drive that day. The truck had an air-conditioner, but it drew too much power and slowed them down too much to use. The wood gas-fueled engine wasn't as efficient or powerful as when they'd used the diesel fuel, which they had long since run out of.

Adrian was cooking a huge rattlesnake for dinner.

"I kind of thought you were kidding about eating rattlesnake back in Corpus," said Ryan, "but here we go again. How many does this make, five or ten thousand that we've eaten?"

Adrian replied, "Exactly seven. This makes the seventh. We've actually eaten a lot better than I expected. The Javalina population is pretty good; besides, rattlesnake is damn tasty, tastes just like chicken."

"The hell it does." Jose piped in. "It doesn't taste anything like chicken...but it's not bad."

"Time to radio in." Adrian said changing the subject. "Whose turn is it?"

"Yours." Ryan and Jose said at the same time.

"But I'm cooking."

"Doesn't make any difference, it's your turn." Jose said with a smile.

Adrian didn't mind radioing in, it was generally a quick report. This one wouldn't be more than just a check in. They'd had some interesting news to send in the past few days, but nothing today. They had recruited five spies so far. He climbed into the truck, pulled out the radio and hooked it up, then pushed a button and listened while the antenna rose ten feet into the air. Turning on the radio he called in.

"Base one this is mobile one, over."

"Mobile one we read you, over."

"We're doing fine here, making progress, nothing else to report, over."

Then the half-bored sounding operator was replaced by the Admiral's voice. This was the first time the Admiral had responded directly. *Uh-oh, this can't be good.* Adrian thought.

"Well I've got something to report." The Admiral said in a strained tone. "You're so-called 'Angels' have captured my ship and I am *not* well pleased."

Adrian sat stunned for a moment. "Excuse me, Admiral? I must have misunderstood you, please say again."

"I said, and I know damn good and well you heard me, *the girls captured my ship.* They went out for their maneuvers as they call them. They were gone two very blissful and quiet days. I was up on the bridge on the third night when they came in with guns and told us we were captured. The little demons snuck onto the ship, past all of my security, managed to sneak all the way to the bridge and start a fire in a trash can for a diversion. When everyone was focused on the fire they came in through the hatch and took us prisoner. Over."

Adrian took a deep breath and then said, "Was anyone hurt Admiral, over?"

"Damn it Adrian this isn't funny! They made a complete mockery of our security! And don't think security isn't getting a hell of an ass-chewing over this. I'm completely revamping how we secure the ship, it's a total cluster-fuck damn it. Over."

Adrian couldn't think of a thing to say. He was torn between being upset with the girls and being proud of them.

"Adrian? Answer me." The Admiral was too furious to continue using radio protocol.

With a mighty effort, Adrian pulled himself together and tried to sound serious. "Sorry Admiral, the signal grew weak there for a minute. What is it you want me to do? How did they get on board without being seen? Over."

"The little brats climbed up the power cables. Do you know how fucking dangerous that is? Every one of them, even the littlest, crawled right up those cables."

Adrian waited a beat making sure the Admiral was waiting for a response. "My deepest apologies Admiral, I'm sure you're plenty upset and rightfully so. What can I do to help? Over."

"I want you to give Race a good old fashioned ass-chewing, that's what I want you to do. Here she is. Start talking."

"Race? You there? Over."

"Yes sir. Oh...over."

Adrian could hear the pride in her voice, even

over the radio and in those two words. "Race, this isn't what you're supposed to be doing. Besides, it's damned dangerous climbing those cables. What the hell were you thinking? Over."

"We made safety harnesses out of rope Adrian, no one could have fallen. It was safe. I decided that we needed realistic infiltration training. We came up with the plan and practiced on it. Then we did it, and Adrian, we did it damned well, too. Oh, and the guns were unloaded. Uh, over."

Adrian finished chewing Race out and instructed her to quit disrupting the ship's routines. After signing off with a still very upset Admiral, he turned off the radio and exited the truck, laughing so hard he could barely walk. Jose and Ryan looked at him as if he'd lost his mind.

"What the hell Adrian? You losing it on us?" Ryan asked, perplexed.

"Wait til you hear this!" Adrian managed to gasp out. When he got his breath back he explained what the girls had done and the Admiral's less-than-pleased reaction. All three of the men then laughed until their sides hurt.

Wiping his eyes, Adrian said, "Well the Admiral has met his match, that's for sure." Starting the laughter all over again.

Two days later Adrian, Ryan, and Jose were sitting around a kitchen table with their host Reynaldo. They had spotted the ranch earlier that day and drove up to the ranch house, a medium-sized frame dwelling, and stopped at a distance. Adrian honked the horn three times to alert the inhabitants, waited a short interval for the inhabitants to look them over, and then stepped out of the van with his hands in the air.

There was a cautious introduction phase as Reynaldo, armed with a shotgun, assured himself that these strangers meant no threat to him or his family. Reynaldo, along with his wife and three young children, had a subsistence farm better than any Adrian had seen so far. They were far enough from any dense population center that they hadn't been run over by the walking starving when the grid dropped. This was remote, near-desolate country. Except for losing the luxury of electricity, their lives had not been strongly impacted.

Adrian took a sip of goat's milk and thought, *This is pretty good. Probably very nutritious, a great survival food.* Adrian said, "Thank you again for your hospitality sir."

"Please call me Reynaldo. Only the police ever used to call me 'sir,' makes me nervous." Reynaldo spoke English with a heavy accent. He was fluent, but the accent sometimes made him hard to understand. "You are most welcome; we get so few visitors that you're a delight to have. I understand what you are saying about an invasion. I've heard much about it. My cousin Juan just came up from Oxaca and has many stories. I sent my son to go bring him here to talk to you about this. He knows much more than I, so we wait for him."

Reynaldo's wife served an excellent lunch while they were waiting. Corn tortillas wrapped around spicy goat meat and pinto beans, and a side dish of cooked greens that Adrian didn't recognize but found delicious, all served again with goat's milk. Adrian asked about the greens and Reynaldo told him they were Moringa leaves. After lunch, Reynaldo took the three men on a tour around his ranch. Adrian told Bear to stay by the truck. The wolf curled up in the shade of the truck and waited patiently.

Goats were the perfect livestock for this arid area, able to survive and even thrive, on the native vegetation. Reynaldo had a windmill that pumped water into a series of tanks. This water kept the goats nearby, and hand feeding them with corn twice a day kept them tame, thus no fences were required except around his corn and vegetable patch to keep the goats out. Reynaldo explained that he planted the corn first and when it was the right height he planted beans around the corn stalks. Once the beans started climbing the corn stalks he then planted squash as well. It was a symbiotic relationship between the plants, each providing something the other needed whether it was shade or something to climb on or nutrients.

"We call them *Tres Hermanas*." Reynaldo said. "It means 'Three Sisters' in English. They work together in many, many ways, and if tended well, bring us great bounty. It is as old as our people."

Adrian was thoroughly impressed. He had never heard of or seen this system before, but then again, he wasn't a farmer. He intended to report this back to the Admiral and ask him to broadcast this information by clear communication to the ham-net so that other people could learn of it. He didn't know it at the time, but the word would spread rapidly and be adopted all over the country.

"Reynaldo, what kind of trees are those?" Adrian asked while pointing to a small grove of trees he had never seen.

"Those are the Moringa trees, *señor*, the leaves we ate are from them. They come from India and grow very well in dry country—they can go a long time with no rain. We eat the leaves and the seeds and the flowers, even the bark can be used. The roots, too, but only a little. The roots can make you sick if you eat too much but they make a good seasoning, like...horseradish. The tree is very strong food, makes us very healthy and strong. I bought the seeds from a man that was travelling through the area selling them. He said the tree has enough food to live on without anything else. He said the tree has more vitamins and other good things than any other plant on the earth, and that they are easy to grow. I took a chance and bought the seeds and planted them and he was right. The trees, they grow ten feet per year and have many branches if the tree is pruned back each year. Much food from these trees, they are a blessing."

As they were walking back to the house Reynaldo's son and a handsome young Hispanic man appeared out of the brush. Reynaldo introduced his cousin, "This is Juan Zuniga, my cousin from Oxaca."

Adrian shook his hand and smiled. Juan returned the shake with a firm grip, something Adrian knew was unusual for the culture, and a small cautious smile. Adrian said, "Happy to meet you Mr. Zuniga."

Juan replied with a bright full smile to this, "Please, just Juan. Thank you."

They all returned to the house and sat around the

kitchen table. Adrian asked Juan what he'd heard about plans for an invasion by the cartels.

Juan nodded somberly, and said, "It is everywhere in Mexico, wherever I went, there is talk of conquering the *yanquis*. They have always seen the United States as a rich paradise, and they still think it. The *cartellistas* are joining up into an army, perhaps thousands are going to come together to move north. Many who talk will not come, talk is cheap and the trip is hard and dangerous. It took me many months to walk from Oxaca to here, many hard times on the way. But many will come for they have nothing where they are, these are hard men, *señor*, very hard men. They will come and take what they want. Much killing will happen."

Juan's English was only fair, he referred to Reynaldo often for the right words.

"Can you guess how long before they get here?" Adrian asked.

"I don't know *señor*. Some have already started, some are waiting to see what happens before they come. I think maybe two months before they get to the border, maybe less, maybe more. I think the first will be many hundreds, maybe a thousand, maybe more. If they are successful, the word will travel back and then many many thousands will come."

"How well are they armed Juan?"

"Oh, very well *señor*. They have many guns, many bullets. They were rich from the drug smuggling and have many guns. The others that follow, maybe later, not so many new guns but many old guns."

"Do you know where they will cross the river at? Have you heard anything about that?"

"Sí. Ciudad Acuna, it is spoken of often as the center. I think they will cross there."

Adrian knew from his map that Ciudad Acuna was the sister city of Del Rio, a week's drive from their present location. "How sure are you of this?" Adrian asked.

"No one can be sure *señor*, but it is said often. I think it is so."

"So in summary you believe that up to a thousand heavily armed former cartel soldiers will be invading Texas near Del Rio within two months, is that about right?"

"Sí, that is what I think. I have walked all the way from Oxaca, deep in south Mexico, to here. I hear much, I say little, I listen. I think when I get here I warn Reynaldo that we must move very far north, maybe to Canada. This is going to be very bad. It will start maybe slow, but will get bigger as the stories go back to Mexico of easy food and riches. The people have nothing and will dream of being fat and rich and will come. They will tell their neighbors and friends and those will tell others and so it will spread quickly. They have nothing so they have nothing to lose. They will come, and it will be very bad. *Muy malo, mucha muerte.*"

As the three men were leaving Reynaldo handed Adrian a small bag, weighing about five pounds. "These are Moringa seeds *señor*. When you go home, plant them. They are very important food."

CHAPTER 17

I N FORT BRAZOS, TEXAS, COLONEL Linda Fremont was meeting with the elected town council: Roman, Sarah, Matt, Perry, and Tim. Linda put her cup of hot tea back on the table after a careful sip. Linda was a Colonel in the Fort Brazos Militia, formed to fight a large band of raiders, she was widowed and had a young son, Scott. Adrian had led the militia to a successful battle that ended the threat. The raider's commander, Rex, had been a personal enemy of Adrian's and Adrian had eventually killed him in an unusual way. Roman and Sarah were Adrian's Uncle and Aunt and had raised him as one of their own after Adrian's parent's had died when he was at a young age. Matt, Perry, and Tim were old friends of Romans and had come to live in Fort Brazos shortly after the grid had dropped. Perry was formerly a lawyer and Tim an engineer. Matt had been an engineer also, and had become the town's blacksmith and preacher. Perry had written a constitution for the Fort Brazos settlement and had become the local judge while Tim had become the town's law enforcement officer.

"I had a ham stolen from my smoke house last night," she said. "I've heard of chickens being stolen and other smoke houses broken into. I hope it's not one of our villagers, or even worse, more than one of our villagers. That would be sad, because there isn't a soul in this town that isn't willing to help each other, there's no need to steal from each other. But it could be one of ours doing it. It could also be that we're getting hit by outsiders, someone living out in the brush and sneaking in. Not that I condone it, but I would almost prefer it. Stealing food is stealing life, it can't be tolerated. We have to find a way to do something about it."

Tim said, "I've investigated most of these recent thefts and whoever it is, he's careful not to leave a trail. He either hits during a rain storm that wipes out his traces, or waits until the ground is dry enough not to leave a trace. I'll get Frank and his coon hound and see if his dog can pick up a trail from your place—it's possible he left a scent. Frank will be here shortly."

Roman drummed his fingers on the table top distractedly. After a pause in the conversation he said, "I hate a thief worse than anything. If it's a villager he'll be banished. We can't banish non-villagers though as by definition they're already living outside our group. Tim, what exactly do we do if we catch outsiders stealing from us?"

"We have the full range of options that our imaginations can come up with." Tim said thoughtfully.

Perry interjected, "That's correct, we can do anything we need to. Outsiders are not protected by our rules since they don't live here. What we want to consider is functionally stopping the thefts, not punishment for the purpose of correcting errant behavior. With a villager we want to mete out a punishment appropriate to the crime with the intent of reconstructing the offender's behavior in such a way that the citizen earns full and complete participation in the community and the trust of the community. With an outsider we just want the stealing to stop."

"That could take many forms. We could simply execute him, and since he's not a citizen a trial isn't required. Strange as that sounds but we only have a very localized government, anyone outside of our jurisdiction, so to speak, has no rights or protections. Only if there was an overall government would that be the case. We could also just run him off with a warning, or we could bring him in as a prisoner and put him to work to make restitution and then run him off. Problem with that is we would end up feeding him more than he stole to start with, not very productive for us, and it would take too much manpower to guard him."

Tim said, "I hear Frank now. Anyone want to come along with us?"

"Damn right I do." Linda exclaimed. "I want to be part of whatever we do if we catch him, I can't afford to be losing good food that way, and I'm pissed off."

Linda asked Sarah, "Would you mind keeping an eye on Scott for me? I'm not sure how long we'll be gone and I don't want him on this trip, too dangerous."

"Of course! He's a joy to take care of, brightens my day to have him around. If you're gone overnight, don't worry about him, I'll take good care of him."

"Thank you Sarah, you are a true blessing to us." Turning to Scott she said, "Now you mind your Aunt Sarah just like you mind me—no mind her better than you mind me, and make yourself useful, take care of her chores while I'm gone." She gave him a hug then a playful swat on the bottom as she turned to follow Frank and his hound.

Linda, Roman, and Tim followed Frank to Linda's smokehouse. Frank led his dog on a leash and walked around to the back of the little wooden building. Frank said, "If I was going to steal a ham, I'd come out of the woods yonder and keep the smokehouse between me and the big house, to keep from being seen. I'd come from the closest spot, too, walking in a straight line. I'll take Brownie here and cut back and forth across that line, see if she picks up anything. If she does I'll take her across it a few more times 'til she gets the idea that I want her to follow the trail. Y'all stay back a-ways at first so she isn't distracted."

Frank led the dog beyond the smoke house and began working a zig-zag path towards the woods, hopefully crossing the thief's trail with each zig and zag. Linda watched and saw that Brownie was getting more excited each time she crossed what Frank had assumed would be the thief's path. In less than five crossings of the trail the dog was straining at the leash, trying to get back to the trail whenever Frank took her over and past it. Frank waved them to follow and then let Brownie follow the trail into the woods. She was straining at the leash, pulling hard while snuffling at the scent.

Brownie raised her head to let out a trailing howl

but Frank hushed her quickly. "Now Brownie, no talking. We don't want this critter to hear us coming, alright girl?"

Linda was amazed that Brownie obviously understood Frank's instructions. *That's one damn smart dog, understands English.* Brownie snuffled and grunted and even growled but didn't let loose with her full voice or bark. Linda had heard Brownie howl more than once when on a trail and she had a beautiful deep voice. It always gave her pleasure to listen to it, but Frank was right—they didn't want to announce their presence miles ahead of time.

Brownie trailed the thief for several hours, not losing the trail or hesitating. Linda and the other men followed, all carrying slung rifles and holstered pistols. They had brought along a pack of food and two tarpaulins for shelter if needed. Tim carried his pack easily, even at sixty plus years he was in excellent condition. Roman and Linda carried the canteens. Frank carried one of Matt's converted shotguns that were designed to instantly kill the largest of wild boars with just one shot. He was a tough old hunter, used to long trails in the deep woods, and not a man to trifle with. His shotgun, loaded with slugs, never left his left hand and the dog's leash never left his right.

Two hours before sunset, they were crossing a creek when a shot rang out and they dove to the ground. Frank was quickly back up and scrambling for cover with the rest of them when another shot from a different spot cracked the air.

"Found them." Frank said ruefully as they all hunkered behind cover. "At least two of 'em, anyway."

Lind asked with concern, "Are you hit?"

"Yes'm, but only a scratch across my arm. Lucky thing, not bad at all."

Tim said, "Tie your dog off, Frank, so she doesn't get hit when we go after them. They'll want to shoot Brownie so they can escape. I'd rather not see that happen. Or maybe it's best if you stay here or go back."

"I'll tie her off," Frank replied tightly. "No son-of-a-bitch shoots and me and gets away with it—hand me a canteen and I'll fill her a bowl of water and leave her some food." With that Frank pulled two bowls and a package of dog food from his own pack. He made Brownie comfortable then told her, "Stay still and be quiet, I'll be back soon." Brownie laid down and curled up comfortably.

Once again Linda was amazed. *Brownie understands and minds better than Scott.*

"Linda," Tim continued, "you and Roman move to the left, try to spot and neutralize the man that fired from your side. Frank and I'll go right and do the same. If anyone gets into trouble, sing out."

Linda said, "Roman let's go over there and spread out about thirty yards and cross the creek in a rush at the same time, then join up again across the creek and work our way up the hill single file with me in front. When we spot our man we'll spread out again, depending on the terrain, and get him in a cross-fire. Assuming the asshole hasn't run away."

Roman whispered, "They won't run knowing we have a trail dog, they have to stop us right here. Okay, let's go."

They crawled into separate positions, spotting good crossing points for themselves. Linda looked over and saw that Roman was ready, she gave a hand signal and they burst out of the woods running, splashed across the creek and dove into cover again. Two quick shots were fired at them but neither was hit, although Linda heard the sonic crack of a bullet only inches from her ear.

Linda signaled to Roman to join her. He crawled laterally to her, staying under cover. "Okay, now we work our way up the hill, you follow me by a few yards and I'll signal if I see him."

For the next hour they carefully moved up the hill in that fashion. Linda stayed low and took her time. She kept her head below the brush line, occasionally looking ahead from the side of a bush. Raising her head up would be asking for it. The problem with this method was that she had to navigate towards where the shots had come from by memory. She had been anxiously awaiting sounds of shooting from the right where Tim and Frank were but hadn't heard anything. *Apparently they crossed the creek further up, out of sight of their bad guy*

Linda signaled Roman to move up beside her. "I think he's about fifty yards ahead, by that big pecan tree. We'll split here. You crawl around to the left in a semi-circle and try to flank him. I'll move over to the right and do the same. Be careful and stay low. Either one of us gets a bead on him open fire. The other will support."

Roman gave her a thumb's-up and began slowly crawling away to his left. Linda began moving to her right. It was slow, arduous work, and she had to stop several times to pick thorns from her hands and arms. *Crawling looks easy, but damn it's hard,* Thirty minutes later she was in a position where she could see the base of the pecan tree but she couldn't make out the shooter. She inspected the brush under the tree carefully, picking through it visually almost leaf by leaf, looking for anything that didn't belong there. After a long time she thought she saw a hand, but it was deep in the shadows of the brush and difficult to make out in the now-fading light. *Time to do something, anything. It'll be dark soon.*

Trying to determine where the shooter's body would be in relation to the hand she thought she might be seeing, she carefully sighted in and squeezed off a shot. Bingo! *Got him, or at least made him move!* She quickly followed up with two more rapidly fired shots and waited to see if he moved again. She heard another shot from her left. *Roman. He must have him in sight, too.* Suddenly the shooter rolled from the brush and Linda pumped another shot into him, knowing for certain she hit him this time.

The man's body lay still, his rifle had fallen and slid down the slope a few feet ahead of him. Not knowing where the other shooter was Linda didn't stand up, but crawled carefully towards the body. Within minutes she spotted Roman doing the same. They met in the brush in front of the body. As they came together they heard a single shot from well off to their right.

Linda whispered to Roman, "Bet'cha they got theirs, too." A few minutes later they heard Tim shout in the distance "We got ours! If you need help fire a shot."

Linda stood up. It felt good to stand after so long on the ground. She started to shout back to Tim when she heard the crack of a rifle and simultaneously felt a stinging sensation in her leg. Linda and Roman dropped down and got behind cover. Roman looked at Linda's leg. "You're hit. Let me look."

Linda felt the pain and looked down to see blood staining her pants. She pushed the leg over to where Roman could inspect it. He slid her pants leg up to her knee. "Through the outer edge of the calf. Small hole, same size on both sides. It's going to hurt for a few days, but it should heal up okay."

Roman wrapped a clean bandanna around the wound and said, "Keep it as clean as you can until we can get a better bandage on it. I'm going after the guy who shot you. I know where the shot came from, see that small boulder over there by that dead tree? He's behind it, got a glimpse. I'll move around to get behind him, you stay here and keep the boulder covered. Watch for Tim and Frank, they'll have heard the shot and think it was a signal for help so they'll be coming along directly."

Linda nodded her assent and Roman quickly moved off. She lay in the prone position, rifle trained just above the rock. *Damn that stings!*

Roman had been gone fifteen minutes when Linda spotted Tim and Frank coming in from her right. Risking getting shot again, she rose, quickly waving to them, then pointing to the rock before dropping back down. Just as she hit the dirt there was another shot, the bullet buzzing close over her head from the boulder. She had gotten lucky and caught the shooter off-guard. A moment later, she heard Roman's rifle crack and saw brief motion from next to the boulder. Then Roman casually walked to the boulder. *Got him.*

Linda stood and limped towards Roman. Frank and Tim quickly caught up to her, obvious concern on their faces.

"Flesh wound, minor but annoying is all." Linda said calmly.

They arrived at the boulder where Roman was turning over the body. "Look at that, just a kid. Probably only fifteen or sixteen years old." Roman looked distressed.

Linda replied, "He chose his path, shot at me twice trying to kill me. Would've, too, if he'd been a better shot. Don't feel bad about it Roman, his fault not yours. He was old enough to have run away instead of attacking, and the little son-of-a-bitch tried to kill me so damn him. Him or us Roman, him or us. Thank you for taking care of him for me."

CHAPTER 18

THE GIRLS WERE GATHERED IN a semi-circle facing Race. They were wearing their camouflage and had striped their faces with grease mixed with ashes. Each face was striped horizontally exactly the same way.

They're scary enough looking. Race thought.

"Okay girls. We're going to keep calling ourselves Adrian's Angels in public—but from here on we call ourselves Adrian's Rangers in private, as we agreed. He taught us to take care of ourselves, protect each other, hunt food, and be on our own. We're free and independent but only because of him."

Race saw in their faces a fierce pride, a justified pride. "For the next two days we're going to practice scouting and locating the enemy. We'll go out on patrol from here and make a two day loop back. On day three we'll rest and clean up then drive back to the ship."

"Why do we have to go back to the ship?" Alana asked.

"Because we gave our promise to Adrian. We don't need the ship and they don't need us, but we promised Adrian and we keep our promises. Don't we Alana."

Alana nodded somberly, "Especially to Adrian."

She said quietly. The other girls nodded along with her in full agreement. "Especially to Adrian." Another of the girls said.

The next morning the girls were moving by first light. They walked single file through the mesquite brush, spaced as far as they could and keep in sight of the girl ahead. The second oldest girl brought up the rear of the line to make sure the younger ones didn't fall behind. They moved slowly enough to be completely silent and used hand signals for communication.

Race suddenly got a whiff of mesquite smoke and raised her hand to halt the column, each girl in turn raising her hand to signal those behind. She stood for a minute sniffing the air, it smelled fairly close. She signaled a sit-down halt and then moved back down the line checking each of the girls, making sure they had their rifles loaded with one in the chamber and the safety on.

Race chose Lila and Celia to accompany her and ordered the rest wait where they were. With the two girls behind her she began cautiously working her way through the brush following the smell of what she thought must be a campfire. *Excellent, a perfect training opportunity to practice reconnoitering an enemy position.*

As she moved towards the smell she eventually spotted smoke curling up from a low spot nearby. She and the two girls moved closer to the smoke, constantly stopping and scanning every opening through which they could see. She was looking for guards, but found none. When they had gotten close enough to hear muffled voices they advanced by crawling. They crawled fifty yards before seeing the camp. Watching for a few minutes and looking for guards the girls slowly and silently crept up to a position from which they could see the camp clearly.

Three men were moving around the campfire. It was a long-term camp, apparent by the amount of debris the men had scattered around it. Two tents stood back of the fire a short distance. The men were bearded and had long shaggy hair, wore filthy clothes and showed no outward signs of being interested in hygiene. Animal remains near the fire suggested that they were living by hunting, and little else. Race didn't want anything to do with men like these, yet she was completely unafraid of them. As long as she had her rifle she was at least equal to them, possibly superior given her training.

She could now clearly hear the men talking. "Time to go huntin." One of the men announced as he picked up his rifle. Another man said, "I'll wait here, don't feel like hunting today. Stomach's not right."

The second man picked up his rifle and snarled at the sick man, "Do your business further off than yesterday, and do it upwind this time damnit."

The two men with their rifles slung over their shoulders began walking out of camp towards Race.

Damn the luck. They'll walk right up on us in a second. She whispered to the other girls, "Safety's off and fingers on the trigger, but don't shoot unless I do." She took her own rifle off safety as she said it.

When the men were twenty feet away Race quickly rose to her feet, followed by the two girls. "Hold it right there mister," she said in a completely calm voice.

The two men were startled and began to un-sling their rifles. Race raised her voice this time and said, "Freeze! One more twitch and I start shooting."

"Why, hello, darling! Now isn't this a sweet surprise?" the first man said after freezing like a statue.

"Hell, no, it's no surprise. Been watching you for a while now. You two put your rifles down on the ground slowly and without getting anywhere near a trigger and you might get to live to see tomorrow." Race recognized the look of growing lust on the men's faces and was disgusted.

"Now sweetheart, don't get excited. We'll do just as you say." Moving slowly the two men lowered their rifles to the ground and let go of them.

"Holler at your man by the fire to come on up here, unarmed." Race commanded.

When the three men were standing together Race said, "Move over there by that mesquite tree and stand real still. Walk slow and keep your hands on top of your heads." The men grudgingly complied. This moved the men far to one side.

"Lila, pick up their rifles, get the one in camp and check in the tents for more. Could be more men in there so do it carefully. Bring all their guns back. Don't hesitate to shoot if you have to, and shoot to kill."

The lead man cleared his throat and began to speak, but Race cut him off at the first syllable. "Shut up. You have nothing to say that interests me. You just listen with your mouth shut. We're going to leave you men standing right there. We'll take your rifles off a ways and leave them for you to find.

Do not, and let me make this very clear, *do not* try to follow us. If you follow us we'll shoot you down like pigs."

Race's tone of voice and her calm command of the situation made the men stand silent. Taking the rifles with them the girls backed into the brush and disappeared from the men's sight. Race whispered, "You two go back to the team and explain the situation. Start moving them back to the truck at a pace that'll still let you keep security. Tell them that in a little while they'll hear one shot. I'm going to stay here and watch them until they start to move, then I'll fire a warning shot to keep them there longer and I'll double time to join up with you. Remember, move fast but move cautious, we don't want to run into anyone else by being careless. Now go!"

Race moved laterally so that she wouldn't be where the men last saw her and lay down. She crawled to a spot that gave her a clear view of the men but they couldn't see her. The men waited ten minutes then started to move to where the girls had disappeared. After the first couple of steps she fired, hitting the dirt in front of them. They rapidly moved back to the tree and stood still. Race backed up far enough to be out of sight and trotted after the girls.

She caught up to them an hour later and called a halt and told the girls to gather around. She had been thinking about what Adrian would do in this situation. *Never ever underestimate your enemy,* he had often said. Applying that rule, she had considered while she ran what she would do if she were the leader of the men, what his motivation would be, his strengths, and the skills at his disposal.

"Here's what I think," she said to the gathered girls in a low voice. "I saw the look on that man's face. Lust, pure lust. He was thinking that there really must be a God, to deliver women to him in the wilderness. He's not likely to give up just because we stalled him once. He'll be thinking we're just girls and we had the drop on him, but he can outsmart us and take us easily. These men are obviously skilled hunters, meaning they can track well, they'll follow us for a bit. We left a trail a blind man could follow anyway, plenty of footprints, broken branches, stuff like that. But they won't just follow us, once they get a bearing on which way we went, they'll circle around and get ahead of us and set an ambush. They'll move fast, too. If I'm right, we're going to have to deal with these apes pretty soon."

The girls listened silently, nodding in agreement at Race's assessment of the situation.

"They have the advantage of being able to move fast, of knowing the terrain around here intimately. They hunt it all the time, they know every bush and tree. We have advantages, too, they think there are only three of us. *They're* underestimating *us*, an advantage we have. We also know the terrain that we've crossed to get here. We could circle out and come back to the truck from a different direction, but that would give them enough time to find the truck and set up their ambush there."

Race paused, thinking for a moment. "Here's what we'll do. We'll head back to the truck following our back trail, knowing that they will lie in ambush for us at some point. There are three likely places for an ambush along that way. We can't count on them using one of those spots, we'll have to move as though it could come anywhere at any time. But, I'm betting they'll use one of the three. I'll take the lead, I'm going to move well out in front and watch for them. Lila, you'll be my second. If they hit us before I expect, the rest of you follow Lila's orders. She knows the tactics to use: basically stay out of sight until you have them in a cross fire and then come in slow, taking full advantage of cover, and shooting with full control—target shooting from cover. Three other girls will circle around where they'll be out of the line of fire but to their most likely line of retreat and pick them off if we flush them out."

Lila nodded, and the rest of the girls looked confidently from Race to Lila.

Race continued. "Each time we come to one of the likely ambush spots we'll follow the same basic plan: clear the spot and move on until we find them. You two," she said, pointing to Helen and Regan, "bring up the rear. Stay back a hundred yards and keep a sharp eye on our back trail in case I guessed wrong. If you see them, fire off one shot and run up to us as fast as possible. If that happens, we'll spread out in a semi-circle and wait for them."

"Okay, Rangers, is that clear?" She looked at each girl in turn, looking for signs of confusion or doubt. She was met each time by clear eyes, excited eyes. These girls weren't just ready for the coming action they seemed eager for it. She recognized what Adrian had told her once. *"When soldiers train, train hard, train for a long time, train with discipline to go into combat, they eventually become eager to actually do it. That's one of the principles of training soldiers, to get them to a point where they want to go into combat and test their skills.*" She saw he was right, these girls were actually eager to encounter this enemy.

She almost felt sorry for the three men. Almost.

"Let's move out. Give me a five minute head start." Race rose to her feet and moved down the trail.

CHAPTER 19

RACE MOVED AHEAD SWIFTLY AT first, then settled down to a slower pace. She moved from cover to cover at a dead run, zig-zagging as she went, scouring the brush ahead with intensity between each move. It was a run, pause and scrutinize, then run again action. In this brush, a man could hide fairly easily. She was taking as few chances as she could.

She continued in this way until she had nearly reached the first ambush spot the men might use. Given the amount of time since the men would have started, she didn't think it had high odds of being the place. It was, however, not something to bank on and would be a good rehearsal for the girls for when they did encounter the actual ambush spot.

She waited until the rest of the Rangers caught up to her.

"Remember that little knob up ahead?" she asked the girls. "That's ambush spot number one. There are some small boulders up there they can lay behind that give them a good view of the trail and a good field of fire. We'll call that knob the center of a clock dial. We're at six o'clock right here." She pointed to six of the girls, "You're Alpha Team, move around to ten o'clock." Pointing to six other girls, "You're

Bravo Team, move to eight o'clock. The rest of you are with me, we'll move up to twelve o'clock, it'll take us a bit longer to get into position. Everyone check your watches. Okay, team leaders, we move on ambush point number one in exactly thirty minutes. Don't shoot unless you have a target and take your time to shoot accurately. We'll meet up on the knob. Move out."

Forty five minutes later the girls had all arrived at the top of the knob. There had been no sign of the men.

"Well done, very well done." Race said with obvious pride. "That clears ambush point number one. We'll do the next one in the same way. There's a draw about a mile ahead that we walked through, that's spot number two. I'll be ahead and let you know before you get there."

Race took the lead and repeated her previous pattern. Watching, then running zig-zag to the next cover. She ran bent over and as silently as possible. Each time she left cover she found she was holding her breath and didn't breathe again until in the next cover. She was tense, feeling that each time she moved she had a rifle lined up on her. The tension was exhausting. She was in excellent physical condition but mental tension also fatigues the muscles. She thought the rest of the girls would be just as tense, especially the rear-guard. She considered taking a break when they came together again, but decided against it. She wanted to get to the truck before dark and at their current rate of travel it would be a close thing.

At ambush point two the girls repeated the maneuver to secure the location. Still no sign of the men. Race said to the girls, "Alright then, there's one more likely ambush spot. If they're not there then we have to assume they'll be anywhere along the trail or already at the truck."

As Race approached ambush point three, another knob, higher than the first and covered with brush and boulders, she noticed that she was nearing total exhaustion. The constant tension was draining her fast. Taking a swig of water she waited for the girls to catch up to her.

"This could be it," she said softly. "Let's take five minutes' rest, but stay alert and face outwards in a circle. Drink a lot of water and eat a protein bar. If they're up there, it could take a long time to finish them off and you can't be moving around and sloshing canteens."

Five minutes later she said, "Team leaders check your watches. It's going to take longer to get into position on this one so we'll move in on it in exactly one hour. Move out."

As the girls infiltrated the brush Race was proud of how silent they were and how quickly they melted out of sight. The girls had the natural advantage of being short-statured, allowing them to stay out of sight by crouching only a little as they moved. The youngest girls didn't even have to do that, but did anyway, their training and discipline showing.

Race said to Lila and Selena, "Remember, our job is to catch them when they flush. Unless we have good, clear shots we don't want to shoot. We want them to run away from the other girls and expose themselves, then we shoot."

Forty minutes later Race's team was in position. She could see the knob clearly, but didn't see the men. If they were up there they were well-hidden. She knew their hunting skills would make them serious adversaries in these conditions. Now it was watch and wait.

Five minutes before the hour was up, Race noticed a mockingbird start to land on one of the taller mesquite bushes on the hills. Just before it landed it swerved away and flew off out of sight. *Gotcha, you rotten sons-of-bitches.* It was another thing that Adrian had taught them: *"Watch the wildlife, they will often show you where someone is hidden."* She knew the bird had spotted something just before it settled onto the branch and swerved-off in startled flight.

Adrian had also told them that combat was often long, boring, tense hours followed by short minutes of intense action. *"The trick is to keep your mental focus both while bored and when the action suddenly starts. Losing mental focus has gotten more people killed than anything else,"* he'd said on several occasions. Race had only today realized just how hard that was to do, but she'd be damned if she'd be caught drifting. That constant focus was also draining. But the sight of that bird taking off had ramped up her adrenaline to a heart pumping height.

She whispered to her team mates, "They're by that tallest mesquite. Be ready, the action will start in a few minutes. I'm changing the procedure a bit though. As soon as I think Alpha and Bravo teams are nearing the target we're going lay down a barrage at the base of that tree. That'll signal the other teams that this is a hot spot and to be careful. It'll also distract the men so they'll be looking towards us and not where the teams are coming in from. Spread out, twenty yards either side of me and fire when I do."

Race imagined the scene as though from the air. She mentally pictured where the girls were, how fast they were approaching, the field of view the men had—she was sure they were focused on the trail below—and where they would be waiting in ambush.

Waiting for the two teams to get close enough to be effective was a long, tense, and seemingly eternal time. She itched to start firing, but didn't want to go too soon, or too late. Finally, with one last glance at her watch she took careful aim at where she thought a man would be likely to be hiding and slowly squeezed the trigger. The gun roared, surprising her with how loud it was. She hadn't realized how quiet it had been. Immediately following her shot were two more. Race wanted desperately to pump bullet after bullet into the bushes up there but with steely determination waited instead, looking for movement.

There! She aimed and squeezed off another round immediately. More motion. Now she was on automatic pilot, looking for signs of movement and firing at it, waiting then doing it again and again. She was barely conscious now of the sound of her rifle or the loud cracks from her teammate's rifles.

Then she heard a shot from across the hill. *They've spotted them and are moving in.* She was elated and filled with trepidation at the same time. *Be careful Rangers, be damn careful.*

The men were firing back now. Race didn't know

if they had actual targets or not, but none of the fire seemed to be coming anywhere near her. When they shot, she could see dirt and dust scattered by their muzzle blasts. Using those as cues she sighted behind where the dust flew up and fired three quick rounds each time. Now the firing from the girls had settled down, brief blasts followed by silence then more brief blasting.

Suddenly one of the men jumped to his feet with his hands in the air. Race and several others shot him immediately. *Bad move asshole, we were all on hair trigger. You should have shouted your surrender not jumped up with a bunch of adrenaline-charged shooters around you.*

Now the question in her mind was whether the other two men were out of action or lying in wait. After the man had fallen, the firing had stopped. No firing was coming from the hill and the three teams were waiting to see if the men were dead or not. Race signaled her teammates back to her.

"We're going up the hill. Advance and cover just like we drilled. Get ready." Race then yelled out loudly "Team Alpha and Team Bravo! Maintain your positions and hold your fire, we're coming up the hill. I repeat we're coming up the hill."

To her teammates she said in a normal tone of voice "I hate to let those men know we're coming, but I'd hate it worse if an overexcited Ranger took a shot at us by mistake. I'll dash to that spot there, while I do each of you fire one shot into their position to keep their heads down, don't fire at the same time though. Then I'll do the same as you come up to me. When you get up to me we'll do it again. I'll take the lead on each jump. Ready? Let's go."

When Race was finally in position, she saw that two of the men were clearly dead, but she wasn't certain of the third one. He'd been hit at least twice from what she could see. The other two were riddled with bullet holes and were both lying face up. The third, the leader of the trio, was face down. Carefully and quietly she approached, keeping the man covered and her finger on the trigger ready to shoot.

When she was within two paces she could see that he was still breathing, a wheezing sound coming from his chest. His hands were in clear sight and his rifle had fallen out of reach. She considered shooting him in the head to finish this off, but she wanted him to see it coming if he was conscious, so she and two other girls rolled the man over onto his back.

He looked up at her and weakly spat out "Bitch!"

She looked into his eyes for a long moment, then said "Who's the bitch here?" and shot him between the eyes with grim satisfaction.

None of the girls had been injured, they had maintained strict discipline and not exposed themselves to fire. The men had been firing wildly, having been given no targets.

"I'm proud of you beyond any words I have to express myself," Race told the girls. "You were perfect, just beautifully perfect. Adrian would be proud of all of us, his training has made us what we are. We are Warriors by God! Adrian's Rangers!" She shouted, lifting her rifle high over her head.

"*Race's Rangers!*" the girls shouted back at her at the top of their lungs. Race started to object, but the girls overrode her with their shouting. They shouted it over and over in perfect unison, pumping their rifles up and down as they bled-off the intense adrenaline high from the combat.

If the girls had been solidly bonded before, now they were welded. They had become a well-honed fighting unit, tested and proven, and they were keenly aware of it. They were closer now than any sisters could ever be.

Race's Rangers, Race thought as they shouted. *Why not? Why the hell not?*

With that battle action they became more than just a cult, they became a deadly fighting cult. One that in the future would spread across the country and grow larger with each passing year.

CHAPTER 20

RYAN COMPLETED HIS RADIO REPORT to the Admiral, repeating word for word Juan's story and admonitions, even adding in the information about the Three Sisters and Moringa trees. "If the Three Sisters and Moringa tree check out it, would be a good thing to broadcast so other people can try it," he said

The Admiral replied. "Excellent report men, we're starting to get a much clearer picture now. The spies you sent in are also sending in reports, and they all tally with yours. Del Rio keeps coming up, and soon. I'm afraid they are more advanced in their movements than we had originally thought. The question now is what we do about it. Over."

Adrian picked up the microphone. "I've been thinking about that, Admiral. We're going to need a lot of men, and I have an idea about that. I think it's time to broadcast over clear radio, on the ham-net, what's going on and to ask for volunteers to rally in Cotulla, near Laredo. If you'd get your radio men to send out a distress signal to all of Texas that we need fighters down here as fast as possible, and ask each ham operator to repeat the call to arms, I'm hoping that we'll get enough volunteers to put up a fight. Over."

"Laredo? They're coming at us at Del Rio, Adrian. What's your thinking? Over."

"A couple of things, Admiral. One, there's no doubt the cartel coalition will hear the broadcast. We can't help that, so we might as well misdirect them as much as we can. Let *them* think that *we* think the battle will be at Laredo so they keep heading for Del Rio. Secondly, it will give us time to organize the volunteers and get in some rudimentary training as we move to Del Rio. By the time we get there, our fighters will be at least somewhat organized and disciplined. Over."

"Roger that. Good thinking. We have twelve of your riverboat trucks ready to go. I'm going to send every soldier we can spare down to you with them. They'll be coming in transport trucks, loaded with as many arms and as much ammunition as I can find. They'll be communicating their progress on this frequency so you'll know when and where to expect them. My head count for this expeditionary force is three-hundred men. They'll be under your command upon arrival. Make the best use of them you can. Over."

"Three-hundred?" said Adrian, shaking his head. "I hope we get a good turnout of volunteers, then, Admiral. This isn't Thermopylae; we need a lot more than that, but I'm not complaining. Every fighter we get, we'll be lucky to have, and the arms and ammo too. I look forward to seeing the river boat trucks and how we can use them. Looks like we have maybe six weeks to get our army together, train them, and be in Del Rio to welcome our unfriendly neighbors; lots to do and not nearly enough time. Please start those broadcasts for volunteers tonight if you would. Over. Oh wait, I have another request. Would it be possible to send one of your planes over Fort Brazos to drop off an encrypted radio? I need to talk to our militia there. Over. "

"Will do. I'll have a jet over Fort Brazos in two hours drop a chute with the radio and instructions. We'll start the volunteer request broadcast tonight and repeat every four hours until further notice. Over."

"Thank you Admiral. How are the girls doing? Any more bridge invasions? Over." Adrian grinned as he asked the question.

"You may think that was funny. It wasn't. There have been some developments with them. They came back from their latest training excursion this week and they seemed different. They were much more self-contained, and of all things, were quiet for a change. No idle chatter, no goofing around. It worried me, so I had the ship's psychologist have another talk with them. He said that it was almost like trying to talk to POW's. They answered his questions, but didn't elaborate on anything. He said that he believed they experienced some kind of difficulty, but wasn't at all clear what it was. Other than that he gave them a clean bill."

The Admiral paused, very briefly, before continuing, but long enough for Adrian to notice.

"There's something else you should know," the Admiral said. "One of the sailors caught Rylie alone and tried to force himself on her. Over."

"Is she alright? Did he hurt her? I'll kill the son-of-a-bitch when I get back!" Adrian was so angry that he forgot radio protocol.

"No she's fine, not a scratch or bruise on her. We'll court martial the sailor when he gets out of the hospital. Over."

"Some of the men roughed him up did they? Good, very good. Over."

"No Adrian, it wasn't the men. It was Rylie. She cut him up pretty badly...well, very badly actually. Let's just say that he'll have trouble fathering children in the future. Those girls are changing Adrian, they're more...feral...yes, *feral* is the best word I can use to describe them. They look at you and it's like a predator looking at you. It's a creepy feeling Adrian, almost as though they are looking for a weakness just before an attack. That sailor didn't stand a chance Adrian, not a chance. Doc said that the girls are also talking about you differently, as though you had become more of an abstraction now than a reality. Over."

"An abstraction? I don't understand. Over."

"He said that they almost worshipped you when you were with them, but it was the kind of admiration where they saw all of your warts but still admired you anyway. Now he says that with your being out of sight they have forgotten you have warts. It's a form of hero worship based not on reality, but more on idealization. Kind of makes sense I guess. Over."

"Good Lord. All I wanted to do was to see them safe and healthy and settled down someplace decent. I'll have to deal with that when this war is over and I can get back. Tell them I'm thinking of them...hell, go ahead and tell them I love them and miss them. Damned if it isn't the truth anyway. But tell them I also said to mind themselves until I can get back.

And tell them to stick together in groups, don't be getting caught alone like that. Might not work out so well next time. Over."

After Adrian shut off the radio he shook his head over the news of the girls. He mulled over what the Admiral told him, but realized there wasn't a thing in the world he could do about it right now. *Time enough for that later. Assuming there is a later.*

That evening Adrian heard the first of the call-to-arms broadcasts. The Admiral had crafted a good solid message, one that would stir the hearts of the men who heard it, a rousing message that played on a Texan's love of his state. *He all but called Texans back to the Alamo for one last good fight. But he could have left my name out of it.*

His best guess was that any nearby volunteers would start trickling in within a few days. Others would come in for over a month, with six weeks probably being the sweet spot, and by then it would be fighting time. Organizing them would be difficult.

Adrian looked at Ryan and Jose. They were sitting around their campfire after dinner. It was getting late and they would soon be going to sleep. "Gentlemen, I'd say that our mission is complete. I'll be going back to Cotulla to start up the war engine. Once there you two can go on back to the ship. It's been a damned interesting time, and I'll hate to see you go. But we've accomplished our mission and it's time to move on."

Ryan quickly replied, "Are you trying to order us back? Because if you are then you'll have to court martial me for refusing orders. I'm staying. Hell, Adrian, this is a historian's dream. Wars have caused more changes to history than any other type of event. This one...this one has the potential to change the future of our world for centuries to come. It has all the components of a major watershed moment in history. You'll have to shoot me to keep me away, damnit. Even then I'll haunt you."

Adrian opened his mouth to reply, but before he could utter a word Jose jumped into the conversation. "Me too, Adrian, I'm not going back either. A large component of your volunteers will be Mexican Americans, many of whom will not be fluent in English. You'll need me on your staff to translate. Besides, the Admiral didn't order us back—he *did* order us to accompany you. Sorry, but we're following orders passed down through the chain of command. Fact is we can't go back, we'd be disobeying orders if we did."

"Alright you stay," said Adrian, holding up his hands in surrender. Then he grew more serious. "But as ordered by the Admiral, once we rendezvous with the troops he's sending, I'll be your commanding officer per military regulation. I appreciate the fact you want to stay; frankly, I really wanted you to stay, but I had to give you the option of not fighting a Texan's war if you didn't want to."

Adrian gave them a big smile and added, almost jokingly, "Just remember that when I'm your commanding officer, I will absolutely not brook any further attempted mutinies of this sort. Now, I think it's time to break out that bottle of tequila that Reynaldo gave us and toast to the upcoming victory of Texas over the Mexican Cartels."

Sheila Johnson was on duty in the ship's radio room. She and the duty officer, Matt Reynolds, had broadcast the call to arms earlier that evening and listened as it had been repeated over and over. It was soon apparent that the entire globe was tuned in to what was happening in Texas as the word spread rapidly from continent to continent. Sheila had been following Adrian's exploits by radio for over two years, just like nearly everyone in the United States. It didn't surprise her that his story was avidly followed around the world. She had often gossiped with her female co-workers about the romance between Adrian and Linda, and they all eagerly awaited any new tidbit of information.

Shelia and Matt sat in front of the radio panel in their usual silence, each absorbed in their own thoughts. Sheila's console indicated radio traffic on one of the encrypted frequencies and she turned up the sound to listen. She heard Adrian talking, and quickly punched Matt in the shoulder. He took off his earphones to listen.

"...if you heard the radio broadcast calling for volunteers to fight, then you pretty much know what all I've been up to, Linda. Over."

Sheila turned up the volume a little, she didn't want to miss a single word between these two. She would be the gossip Queen for a month!

"We heard it, Adrian. It came as a total surprise, thinking you were down there just looking around before coming home and all of a sudden you're leading Texas in a war with Mexico. I should have known you wouldn't just look around and come back, not you." She laughed nervously before saying "Over."

"Yeah, well...I didn't exactly go looking for this. Kind of still surprises me, too. This is going to be a big war, but the consequences of not fighting it are dire. We have to stop this before it gets going or everyone is going to suffer, and badly. Over."

"I know, I know. You just can't help yourself. It's one of the million things I love about you. We're already gearing up to come down and fight; the entire Fort Brazos Militia will be there, including me. Give us three weeks or so and we'll be together again. Over."

"Speaking of love, Linda, I have a lot to say on that subject, but only one question to ask..."

Sheila was shocked when Matt reached over and turned the sound off. "What the...?" she started to ask.

Matt looked at her with a calm and level gaze, "Some conversations should be private, Sheila. Some things we don't need to listen in on. He requested an encrypted radio sent to her for a reason. He could have talked to her over the open air, but he had something private to talk about. Let them have their privacy; lord knows they deserve it."

Sheila fumed. She knew Matt was right, but she still wanted to listen. "Damn him all to hell and gone, that was going to be juicy."

It took three days for Adrian to get to the rally point outside Cotulla, sixty-eight miles north of Laredo. They drove straight through, stopping only to switch drivers every four hours.

Adrian was driving and the other two were awake

as they crossed over a little river and neared the rallying point. Looking over the guard rails, Adrian saw a camp with what appeared to be at least two hundred tents.

"That was fast." Adrian exclaimed. "Very fast. I didn't expect to find anyone here yet. Damn good sign, I hope."

As they approached the camp, Adrian was amazed to see what he guessed to be four hundred people. As they stopped the truck and dismounted, someone shouted out, "General Bear is here!" They were quickly surrounded by some of the toughest men and women Adrian had ever seen gathered in one place. He wasn't sure he was going to survive the back-slapping and hand pumping that quickly ensued.

Adrian, Ryan, and Jose exchanged a meaningful glance over the heads of the volunteers. They had their work cut out for them, but they just might have a chance.

CHAPTER 21

THE NEXT THREE DAYS WERE a frenzy of activity, with more men arriving daily. They came on foot, on horseback and by a multitude of trucks converted to wood gas and home-made liquid fuels from alcohol to diesel fuel. Adrian was continually amazed at how many were answering the call and their ingenuity in transporting themselves. He was also surprised at the number of women. They hadn't come as camp followers either, they had come to fight

To defend Texas, as he heard over and over. Texas, not the United States of America, but Texas. It was a common refrain. "What did the federal government ever do for us? They knew a solar storm could wipe us out and all they did was keep taking that special interest money. The bastards." Adrian heard it often.

His first action on arrival was to assemble all the volunteers, which was no problem since they had come running when the word spread he had arrived. They eventually settled down under the highway overpass, which Allowed Adrian to climb the embankment high enough to see all their faces. The overpass reflected his voice, making an impromptu amphitheater. It was standing room only with everyone squeezing in tightly. At this point he had a rough head count of four hundred and fifty men and women.

"First I want to thank each and every one of you for showing up. We have a bloody battle ahead of us and I don't expect it to be anything other than extremely difficult. But this is our land and by God no one is going to take it from us!" He shouted the last sentence and was immediately the recipient of loud shouting back from the crowd. He allowed them to settle down a little, then continued; as he did they quickly fell silent to catch every word.

"We'll win by being organized and moving with discipline. We'll be outnumbered. Badly outnumbered. They have more soldiers and more weapons than we do. But we have your courage and we'll be organized into groups that can move swiftly and strike like a rattler."

More cheering erupted, and Adrian again waited a few moments before continuing. He knew they needed this emotional release, and it was an excellent method of bonding them together.

"Other than the fact that they will out-number and out-gun us, we've got 'em licked." Adrian said quietly and with a smile. "Fact is I feel kind of sorry for them, but not so sorry that I don't want to kill every last one of the sons-of-bitches!" His voice rose to a loud roar at the end.

More cheering, and this time laughter mixed in with it.

Adrian waited a beat then continued. "We'll set up several groups to organize this campaign. First we'll create an incoming group. They'll greet new arrivals, interview them and assign them where they'll do the most good. This group will begin by interviewing each of you to find out how you can best help. When they come around give them your full cooperation. Part of what they'll be doing is asking for an inventory of food and arms. We'll have to distribute any extra food and arms as evenly as possible. We'll all need to go on food rationing immediately. Food is going to be one of our biggest problems, it takes a lot of food to feed an army and we don't have supply lines behind us to help. But...neither do they"

Adrian stopped to let that sink in before continuing. "I'll choose unit commanders based on the results of the interviews by an incoming staff and then by personal interviews and any recommendations that anyone might have. From the interview results each person will be assigned to a combat company. Companies will be designated by alphabet such as Alpha, Bravo and hopefully all the way to Zulu."

"Once assigned to a company you'll move to your company area in the camp and begin training as a unit. Your Company Commander will choose his lieutenants and platoon squad leaders, basing his or her decision the same way I base mine. I'll review each Company roster with its Commander and confirm those assignments. Training will cover the basics of ground warfare. We won't bother with the niceties of parade ground drilling, but we will cover the basics of formations and movement and communication. I have a good idea of the tactics we'll use, and we'll train on those extensively."

There was a murmur of approval from the crowd. Adrian continued.

"I'll also create an intelligence branch. Their job will be to monitor the enemy location and disposition and report to me for overall planning. Troops will be assigned to the signal corps for carrying messages, dispatches, and troop movement and engagement orders. We'll also need to establish a medical corps for battlefield treatment of wounds—if you have particular skills in that area, be sure to let your commander know."

"Within a very few days each of you will have your assignment, will know what's expected of you, and you'll know where you're supposed to be and what you're expected to be doing. When the time comes—and it will come very soon—we will progress in an orderly fashion to the battlefield, deploy with discipline and strength and then deliver a very serious and deep ass-kicking."

Once again cheers rang out. It took several minutes for them to simmer down enough for Adrian to ask, "Okay, now let's get the questions and answers rolling. Who wants to go first?"

One man quickly stood and shouted out "General Bear is it true that you slept with a grizzly and gave her babies?"

The crowd erupted into loud laughter and a lot of hooting and general applause.

Adrian had been asked this so many times that he'd finally given up trying to explain the truth, though he'd only recently learned to roll with it. He smiled and waited for the laughter to die down then held up his hand and quickly got silence. "Yes it's true, and I have the scars to prove it," he said unbuttoning his shirt to show the scars that ran from his navel up to his cheek. "That's what home-made whisky will do to you."

At this laughter rang out as some of the men and women bent over from laughing so hard.

Adrian buttoned his shirt back up and as the laughter slowly died he said, "And she keeps calling asking me to come back." This started another round of laughter. Adrian smiled back and waited, he knew they had to get this out of their systems before the real questions would start.

"General, what flag are we going to use?"

This caught Adrian off guard, he hadn't thought about a flag. "Damn good question and one that should be put up to a vote right now. Let's hear suggestions and then vote on them."

"How about that rattlesnake with 'Don't Tread On Me' flag?" someone shouted. A loud cheer went up at this suggestion.

Adrian said "Let's see a show of hands. I'd call that unanimous." More cheering. Adrian asked "Anyone here have the ability to make us a flag like that?" Several people raised their hands. Adrian nodded. "Those of you with your hands up please get together and see what you can do. I think it should also have 'Texas' on it somewhere, don't you?" More cheers. "How about *'Don't Tread On Texas'*?"

Adrian looked up, he didn't think it was possible but it sounded as though the bridge would be pulled down on them from the sheer volume of the cheering.

Adrian fielded a series of routine questions after that. Where to set up sanitary facilities, did he know how many more volunteers would come in, and so on. One woman asked if he was authorized to perform marriages. Adrian replied, "No ma'am, but I'm willing to bet dollars to donuts there's a half-dozen preachers here right now." Several men and women raised their hands to let everyone know they were, indeed, preachers.

"That reminds me," Adrian said, "we also need a Chaplain's Corps. You folks, please see me after the meeting."

After that the rest of the meeting was more subdued as the volunteers imagined the upcoming duties of the Chaplains.

The days blazed by far too fast for Adrian to be comfortable with. Every day new volunteers arrived in droves. Keeping up with getting them interviewed and assigned to their companies was a full time operation in itself, but there was much more to do. Adrian set up training regimens for the company commanders to follow. As soon as the companies were operating with a semblance of order, they would train company to company and then move on to full battle tactics.

He created a Messenger Corps whose duty was to quickly and accurately relay messages to and from the battlefield in case their limited number of radios became an issue. Adrian chose Ryan and Jose to be his Adjutants, his top staff. They were kept in constant motion coordinating the volunteers in their training and assignments.

The men the Admiral sent arrived and everyone was extremely happy to see them. When the river boat trucks arrived in convoy, with the trucks full of troops and tanker cars of fuel, all of the volunteers broke discipline and rushed to greet them. Adrian sent runners to the Company Commanders to allow this break in discipline without punishment. They were volunteers, after all, and some allowances had to be made until they were closer to combat conditions.

Adrian used a stick to point out the features in the terrain model that the intelligence team had made after they had returned from their scouting mission, and pointed out where the cartel was most likely to cross the river. "Here's the plan."

Adrian outlined the plan, talking for half and hour, then asked. "Questions?"

"How sure are we they'll cross at this spot?" asked one of the company commanders.

"About ninety percent." Adrian responded. "We have good, on-the-ground intel coming in and they are still heading towards it. It's about the only decent place for them to cross. Everywhere else has too many terrain issues. We'll monitor their progress and if their direction changes we'll move to meet them."

"Do we have a solid head count on them yet?" asked another commander.

"No, we estimate maybe two thousand of them against our eighteen hundred, but the estimate does not have a high confidence factor. They're well-armed and semi-disciplined. They're on foot with only the four trucks used by their leaders. They may have the numbers; but we have the mobility and the element of surprise. These are not trained military men.

They've never been in combat against a well-armed and determined enemy. But that doesn't mean they won't be hard fighters. If all goes according to plan, they won't be able to organize a counter-attack"

"Damn, I almost feel sorry for them." one of the men muttered.

CHAPTER 22

LINDA TURNED OFF THE ENCRYPTED radio and walked over to Roman's house, where the Fort Brazos Milita was quickly gathering outside. Over half of them were already there.

Roman was among the men talking. When he spotted Linda approaching he called the men to fall into formation.

Linda stopped in front of the men and said, "We've all heard about the Mexican invasion and the call for volunteers. I'll be leaving tomorrow, who wants to go?"

Within two hours all of the militia had come in, men and women alike, and all were determined to reach Cotulla as soon as they could. Linda made a last address to the full contingent

"Pack your things, gather as much food and guns and ammo as you can. We leave in one week, get your affairs in order at home, make arrangements for your children and for neighbors or friends to take care of your place while we're gone. We could be gone for a long time. It's easy to underestimate how long a war will last and we have a long way to travel back and forth and our transport isn't fast."

The volunteers left in small groups, talking excitedly.

Linda turned to Sarah, "Sarah, I need to ask a huge—" but was interrupted by Sarah before she could get the next word out.

"Of course I'll take care of Scott, it'll be a pleasure. He'll keep me company while Roman is off gallivanting around the country. Rest easy on that. Scott will be kept busy with his schooling and chores. He won't have time to worry about you."

"Thank you so much Sarah, I just don't know what I'd do without you."

"It's my pleasure, that little boy is a treasure and I love him like he was my own. It really will be my pleasure, he'll keep *me* busy, too."

The militia pulled out in a convoy at daybreak one week later. They had nearly thirty pickup trucks that ran on wood gas, each truck heavily loaded with volunteers and supplies. They were carrying an enormous amount of food, more than they needed for themselves, knowing that the food would be needed at Cotulla. With the extra loads on the inefficient, wood gas trucks, Linda estimated that the trip would take three or four days if there were no serious problems.

Linda had working CB radios installed in several of the trucks, including hers, and had decided that they would only travel in daylight for security; this meant lost time, but the danger of ambush was tripled at night and fighting in the dark wouldn't be to their advantage against a determined and well thought-out ambush. It wasn't worth the risk. They would still get there in plenty of time. She also had the encrypted radio and talked with Adrian frequently.

Linda turned to Roman, who was riding with her. "I expect that raiders have heard the call, and will be expecting more than usual traffic heading south on the highway. Trucks loaded with things they want to steal. They'll be thinking this is a golden opportunity for them so I'm anticipating roadblocks and ambushes. I'm going to pull ahead of the main body by several miles and act as point, relaying what we see as we go. Do you want to ride point with me, or would you rather not?"

"Drive on." Roman said with a smile. "I'll enjoy being shotgun. But if I may suggest, I think it would be better to have two more trucks accompany us, trucks that have the most volunteers in them. That way, if we hit an ambush, we'll have more firepower to deal with it while the main column catches up. You and I alone could get in pretty deep, too deep for the convoy to come in time to help."

Linda nodded, and picked up the microphone. "This is point to main body. Send the two trucks with the most people in it to follow me on point, we'll have a stronger response to any problems that way."

The militia continued with three point trucks containing a total of twelve volunteers five miles ahead of the main body. Roman noticed on a sharp curve that Matt, Tim, Perry, as well as his own son and son-in-law, along with Adrian's former army squad were in the trucks accompanying them.

He told Linda who was back there, "That was no accident," he said. "I'm guessing they stopped the convoy to switch some people around. Bet'cha that was a Chinese fire drill for the record book."

If they had to stop and wait for the convoy to catch up to them they would have a ten to fifteen minute wait. Once the convoy did catch up to them, the full contingent of 93 volunteers would be in place. Linda didn't expect to find any serious opposition to that number of trained and armed soldiers.

They stopped at noon for a stretch and comfort break and to grab a quick meal. An hour later they were back on the road and traveled uneventfully for several hours.

As the point trucks approached the bridge over the Leon River, Linda caught sight of a flash of light. "Roman, I saw a reflection up ahead beside that bridge. Could be nothing, could be something. I'm going to slow down a bit; keep your eyes peeled."

She slowed down to about half-speed and watched intently.

"That's a good place for a blockade," said Roman. "With the river there, we can't bypass the bridge without going miles out of our way; can't cross the river without the bridge, either. If I was going to set up an ambush, I'd have two trucks hidden on each side of the road on the far side of the bridge and pull them into position at the last moment to block the road, then I'd hit us from both sides. Plenty of trees there to hide as many men as they want to and they can fire from cover. Stop well ahead of the bridge and let's see what happens. We can scout it out on foot, if need be."

"Glad you're on our side Roman, you have a devious mind."

Linda lifted her foot from the gas pedal and let the truck drift to nearly a stop. As she did she radioed to the trucks behind her. "Roman's got an itch and I thought I saw a flash of reflected light by the bridge. We're going to stop short and scope it out before continuing."

The three trucks coasted to a stop a quarter of a mile from the bridge. Linda stepped out of the truck with her binoculars and began carefully scoping the bridge and its surrounds. "Let's move up a bit closer."

They stopped again, two hundred yards from the bridge. As Linda stepped out from the truck she saw a man raising a rifle. Jumping back in she shouted, "Gun! We have to back up."

A bullet hit the door panel at a grazing angle and ricocheted off as she spoke. All three of the trucks immediately began backing up as fast as they could, while men came surging out of the woods ahead of them from both sides, firing rapidly.

Linda knew they couldn't take the time to turn around, and they couldn't back up fast enough. She got on the radio to the other two trucks. "We'll have to stop here. I'm going to turn my truck sideways, you two come up on each side and make a three sided formation to fight from."

As quickly as she could she backed to the right side of the road, then pulled across the road, stopping in the middle with her side facing the oncoming men. She had no more than gotten stopped when the other two trucks pulled up, one at each end of her truck, the three trucks forming a closed triangle. She bailed out behind Roman, and taking cover behind the truck opened fire on the approaching men. Within seconds all twelve of them were firing at the raiders, hitting several of them.

The raiders quickly realized they were the ones in the vulnerable position and ran for the woods on either side of the road, quickly taking cover, but still shooting.

Linda knew the convoy had heard her radio calls and would be coming as fast as they could. She crawled into the cab to get to the radio. "We're taking heavy fire, men advancing on each side of the road taking cover in the trees. By the time you get here they'll be on both sides, front, and rear of us. When we're in sight, stop the trucks and advance on foot along the tree lines. Can't tell how many there are, but it seems like a lot. This could be a long and dirty fight, be ready."

Linda then turned to the closely packed men and women inside the truck-triangle and said, "Our best bet is to stay here until help arrives. Watch your legs, stay behind the tires as much as possible, in case they think to shoot under the trucks."

She had barely gotten the words out when she heard the hiss of air from one of the outside tires, quickly followed by two more. *The bastards are trying to immobilize us so we can't run. They don't have a clue what hell they'll be in shortly.*

Linda picked up the microphone again and said, "We're near mile marker 294, what's your position?"

"Two miles out and closing as fast as we can, figure five minutes and we'll have boots on the ground right behind you."

"Hurry every chance you get, we're take heavy

and sustained fire." Linda dropped the microphone as Roman called out, "They're making a rush on the right!" She looked over and saw that at least a dozen men were coming in fast and firing faster.

"Concentrate fire on those men, but watch the left side, it may be a diversion."

The pace of firing from inside the truck fort picked up rapidly, taking down six men in less seconds. The remaining men turned and ran back for the trees, losing three more.

"Coming in on the right!" Roman yelled.

This group was twice as large, but within seconds they, too, ran for cover under the heavy, well aimed fire, losing eight men. Heavy firing from the trees continued.

Linda shouted out, "Watch for fire from behind us, they'll work their way back there and probably try a rush from all sides next."

The radio crackled. "We're about one minute out, what's your disposition?"

Linda keyed the mike and replied, "Two minor injuries so far. We're still forted-up in the middle of the road and the bad guys are starting to move behind us. Trucks are taking a hell of a beating." As she said that a bullet skipped under the trucks hitting near her foot and banging into the far truck with a solid thud. *Too damn close, we've only got a few minutes before we start taking serious hits.*

It was one of the longest minutes of Linda's life before the convoy crested the far hill. The attackers kept up their fire, but as the trucks came clearly in view began to slacken as they saw the long line of trucks. Linda watched as the trucks stopped a hundred yards behind her and men and women surged out, running for the woods on each side. The firing from the attackers came to a slow halt as they realized the game had just changed. They were now on the defense, something they hadn't expected to happen.

Linda and her team waited as the balance of the militia worked their way through the woods up beside them. When she saw they were even with them, she ordered the group to split in two and rush across the road and into the woods on both sides. "Make it fast, you'll be exposed."

As they quickly rushed for the woods they drew fire, but no one was hit. When they reached the trees she assessed the situation with the squad leaders.

"We have to clear this snake's nest," she said. "Too far to go around, and it would be just plain wrong to leave them here for the next traveler. This is basic advance and cover fighting. One group on each side, meeting at the river under the bridge. The kicker is we have to contain them, not let them take off running up or down the river. They'll take forever to catch if we do, and too many will escape. I want every one of those sons-of-bitches dead before we leave."

Her team nodded in silent agreement.

"Split into two even groups on each side of the highway. One group advance along the tree line to the bridge, the other angle off and take up position up and down river, about three hundred yards from the bridge, who will wait until the runners come at them and mow them down. Questions?"

"Okay, road group give the river groups half an hour to get into position. We move out in forty-five minutes. Get your troops briefed and ready."

At the forty-five minute mark the two roadside groups began moving towards the bridge, one half of each team moved forward under covering fire, then the second half moved forward under covering fire. It was a long and difficult battle, stretched out along the roadside trees, meeting heavy resistance that was hard to dig out because of all the available cover. But when they had nearly reached the bridge, the raiders fell apart and began running. From there it was a fast, run-and-shoot operation.

It took three hours for the militia teams to reach the bridge, then turn and followed the running men until they heard gunfire from their counterparts as the retreating raiders ran into the militia ambushes.

At that point the chasing militia moved forward far more slowly, unwilling to be mistaken for raiders by the forward militia. Linda had to assume that some of the raiders managed to escape, but it wouldn't be very many.

An hour before dark the mop up was completed and the militia had all returned to the bridge. After posting sentries Linda gathered the men and women together. They had killed thirty-eight raiders, and shot all wounded raiders on the spot, per Linda's orders. She wouldn't allow vermin like that to live to raid again.

The militia had lost two and had eight wounded, two seriously.

Linda told the group, "We're going to have to stay here a few days, maybe a week. We have to tend to our wounded, and repair our trucks. Set up camp here; we have the bridge for shelter and the river for water."

The next day Roman walked across the bridge and found two large trucks, ready to block the road. *Thought so.*

CHAPTER 23

D URING WEEK THREE ADRIAN SAID to Jose, "I had an idea last night for transporting our army to Del Rio. Freight train. What if we could get a locomotive into operation. The Admiral sent us six tankers of diesel. We could place one of the tankers on a flatcar behind the locomotive. It starts out as soon as possible clearing the tracks and setting the switches to Del Rio. Then it comes back and we make up a train to carry personnel and equipment."

He leaned over the map and pointed out the route. "We use the tracks that go from here to San Antonio, then over to Del Rio from there. We can carry everyone and everything on one long train, or two shorter ones if we can get two locomotives running. I'm thinking we should be able to make the trip in thirty-six hours, give or take. It's the cleanest and surest way of transporting. The locomotive has to be solidly reliable for this though, last thing we want to do is get everyone stranded far from the action zone."

He looked up at Jose.

"I want you to take personal responsibility for this, see if you can find any railroaders here, find a locomotive, get it running, and clear the tracks of stalled trains. From what I understand of railroads, there should be double tracks every now and then, places where trains can wait while another train goes by. Push them onto those. We want a clear, straight run when we go...assuming you can get a locomotive going."

"It's brilliant! I'm on it." Jose saluted and left on his mission.

Adrian turned then to Ryan. "You wanted to see me?"

"I do Adrian. If you have a few minutes I'd like to talk to you about something critically important."

"Shoot." Adrian replied.

"Let's sit down, this is going to take a few minutes." After they were seated in the camp chairs under the overpass, Ryan continued. "I'm a historian. I have a doctorate in history. It's been my passion since I was a kid, and believe me when I tell you that what I'm going to say...well I've put a lot of thought into it. I've looked it over from every side and came to the same conclusion every time."

Adrian grinned at him, "You might want to tell me what's on your mind then. I'm listening."

"Keep an open mind Adrian because there's a part to this that you might not like, and I don't want you to reject it out of hand. Keep it in mind and think about it for a few days. Watch and listen to everyone in camp and test what I'm going to tell you against their attitudes when they talk to each other. Okay?"

"Okay. What is it?" Adrian asked, wary, but curious.

"Okay, so here goes the prepared speech."

Ryan took a deep breath and dove in.

"There's a desperate need to return to a society of law and order. We came from that society, although it had been rapidly getting to the point where there was too much law and order. It had gotten to the point that no one could get through a day without breaking ten laws. Sorry, I drifted there for a second. The point is now we have no law and order anywhere except maybe in a few, very few, villages such as your Fort Brazos. These people here are the salt of the earth, the absolute best of the best of our society. But there are a lot more people out there that are just plain criminals. They steal and kill without fear because there is no one, no group, to fear."

"I'm with you so far," said Adrian.

Ryan continued. "Right now we have the best opportunity that will come for decades to build a new society based on law again. There are people from every region of the state here right now. Once this war is over and everyone scatters to go home it will be too late; it will be near impossible to gather everyone all together again, not unless another invasion threatens. In order to pull ourselves together, a leader will have to emerge. You are the only real choice for that leader. I don't have to go into what a celebrity you've become. I know it was never your intention, but there it is. I know you don't want to take center stage, stand in the spot light, or become a political leader. But you must. You absolutely must."

Adrian raised his hand up, palm out, to stop Ryan from saying more. Before Adrian could speak, Ryan went on.

"Please let me finish, this is too important for

quick reactions. You've heard the old saying that some people are born to greatness where others have greatness thrust upon them. You're in the second category. From a historian's view, this time, this place, these circumstances, are all working together to thrust you into the front. Just think what you rescued the girls from. They had been there for years and none of the neighboring people did anything about it. You know why they didn't? Because they didn't have a leader, because there weren't any laws, because they didn't think of banding together to do it. But if there had been a bona-fide authority to go to, you can bet someone would have gone to them. It's the same all over the country Adrian. People living without hope of getting any help when the bad guys come. And the bad guys come, Adrian, every day. Right now there are probably several hundred bad guys tearing up good guys, destroying lives Adrian, tearing down what others have built. You've told me about Colonel Fremont's difficulties in getting here, that's going on all over the state right now."

"But right here, right now, we have an opportunity to do something about it. We gather the volunteers, organize them into regional caucuses, have them vote a representative to attend a constitutional convention. They'll agree on a constitution; Perry has one ready to go from what you've told me. We lawfully agree on and sign the constitution and we create a government. These men go home then and spread the word. This new government, with you as its leader, organizes roaming law enforcement groups. They go wherever there is a need and restore law and order. It'll start small and somewhat rough—a little like the Old West, perhaps—but it'll grow over time. This is a watershed moment Adrian. Exactly the kind of moment I've told you about. Either we take advantage of this rare opportunity, or we fail to and everyone suffers."

Ryan fell silent, looking at Adrian with anticipation mixed with trepidation. He was afraid Adrian would reject it out of hand. Adrian looked at Ryan intently, but Ryan couldn't read his face.

"Why does it have to be me Ryan. Why not you, it's your idea. Why not somebody else?"

"That's false modesty Adrian. These people, people all across the country need and want leadership. They crave a stable social arrangement but they don't know how to launch it. Imagine a family that's homesteading far from others. Most people are in that situation. How do they go about starting a country? They can't, they just can't, and you know it. It takes a spark and it takes kindling. You're the spark. Everyone admires and respects you. Everyone knows you; you're the one and only natural leader on the horizon. I've heard a lot of talk about just such things among the volunteers. You listen and you will, too. They are the kindling, all together here in one bunch, ready to burst into flame if you will just provide the spark."

Watching Adrian's face as he talked, Ryan didn't see outright rejection, more of a tired acceptance creeping in. It was time to close the deal.

"With your leave I'll arrange a camp-wide meeting for tonight. I'll propose to them what I've proposed to you. You watch their reactions, and if they don't want this, then you won't have to do it. But they will. I guarantee they'll be ecstatic about the idea."

"So what is it you're proposing exactly?"

"No one out there will go along with restarting the United States. Not one. The only way we can restore a civilized society is to start a new government entirely. I'm proposing we restart the Republic of Texas, but under a new constitution. Later on, other states like Louisiana, Arkansas, Oklahoma, and New Mexico will hear about this new republic and how it's putting things in order. People will start moving to Texas from all over the country when they hear how well it's working. Then other states will begin organizing along the same model. Within a handful of years there'll be a movement towards organizing into a coalition of the new republics. It'll spread, Adrian. The need is great and an example of a working model will encourage others to move in the same direction."

"For the time being it'll not take any of your time. After the war it'll take a little of your time. We need you, Adrian. You have a widespread reputation like Daniel Boone or Davy Crockett had, and that reputation and you're willingness, mixed with the need of these people will make it happen. Nowhere else in America is there an opportunity like this to help people. It would be an absolute crime not to do this."

Adrian sighed. "Call your meeting then. If you're right I'll go along with it, for now. But if we don't win this war it won't matter. Let's get your meeting over with and get back to the real business we have at hand."

The overpass was much too small to accommodate the crowd, so the meeting was held out in the open. Adrian was standing in the crowd and watched as Ryan climbed up onto a hastily erected speaker's platform. The crowd had been noisy, even raucous at times, but as Ryan stood there the silence came slowly at first, then rapidly as they waited to hear him speak.

Ryan, not comfortable speaking in public but knowing that he needed to do this, acted with a confidence he didn't actually have and spoke loudly. "You have a moment in time, a place in history, right now right here...but only if you grasp it quickly. You can let it slip away forever, or you can show your courage and your honor of your fellow Texans by bringing them back two gifts: The first gift will be a resounding victory over the army that intends to invade your land." Loud cheering followed for several moments. Ryan waited, and when he gauged the time was right he held up his hand for silence, which he quickly got.

"The second gift is just as big. Bigger. It's a gift to the men and women of Texas that want to lead their own quiet lives. People who are raising children and want their children, your children and mine someday, to live in a better place than we have now. A place where law and order work for the citizen and against the criminal raiders that scar our land. Gathered here today are the people needed to create a new government, our own government, crafted by our own hands. I'm not talking about resurrecting the United States, or even the state of Texas. I'm proposing that we, right here and now, vote to restore the Republic of Texas under a new constitution."

Ryan paused in the dead silence that followed. For a brief, horrifying moment he thought he had misjudged. He thought they might turn away with disinterest because every face turned to him was silent.

Then one man started to clap. The shock washed away across the crowd as they spontaneously erupted into wild cheering and applause. Men were slapping other men on the back, fists were raised and pumped, a few had tears streaking down their faces. The crowd went absolutely crazy.

Ryan stood above them knowing he had gauged them correctly after all. He looked for Adrian in the crowd to judge his reaction. Spotting him, he saw that Adrian was smiling through the back slapping he was enduring. Ryan knew that as sure as the sun would rise in the morning that Adrian would be President of the Republic of Texas before this meeting ended. Ryan the historian was making his own history now and he knew it, and fully believed it was the right thing to do. *History will judge me for this, I only hope approvingly.* He was fully aware of the irony of a historian being judged for his place in a historic moment.

Choosing the right moment, after the cheering had begun to decrease just slightly but well ahead of anything resembling an orderly crowd, he raised both hands. Slowly the celebrants noticed his call for silence and gradually the crowd settled down, but Ryan knew they were primed to explode again at the slightest cue.

"We'll need to do this in an orderly fashion. First we need to elect the President of our brand new

Republic." Before the crowd could start shouting again Ryan quickly shouted out, "Are there any nominations for the office of the President of the Republic of Texas?"

Ryan knew exactly what would happen next and was not disappointed.

A voice answered immediately, shouting out from the middle of the crowd it said "Bear! Bear! Bear!" His chant was immediately taken up by the crowd. They shouted loud and were soon in unison, shouting "Bear! Bear! Bear!" for nearly ten minutes. No amount of hand raising on Ryan's part slowed them down. When he looked down, he saw that Adrian was being pushed towards the platform by the crowd, they were propelling him forward.

Adrian reached the platform and climbed up. The crowd went even wilder than it had before. Adrian turned to face them and they instantly got quiet again, not wanting to miss a word. Before Adrian could speak, Ryan shouted "I second the nomination, and by voice count I declare that Adrian Hunter, General Bear to his soldiers, is hereby legally and duly elected President of the Republic of Texas!"

It took a full fifteen minutes before the ecstatic crown quieted enough for Ryan to once again speak.

"Before I turn the platform over, there is some quick business we need to attend to. After the meeting tonight we need to meet in smaller groups, groups by region. North Texans meet north of the platform, South Texans south of the platform and so on. Each group will nominate and elect three representatives to act in their behalf in a constitutional convention that will be held as soon as we can. Now...without further delay here is the Father of the new Republic of Texas!" The crowd yet again went wild as he shouted out those last words..

Ryan climbed off the platform leaving Adrian there, alone. He knew the die was cast now, his job done for the time being. He didn't know that at the back of the crowd a ham operator had set up his radio and was broadcasting the meeting across the world, or that the Mexican Cartel leaders were listening with intense interest.

Adrian, when he finally had a chance to speak, said, "I promise to make a short speech if you'll promise to give your throats a chance to rest. They have to be aching by now." Adrian gave a smile and continued quickly, "Ryan sprang this on me earlier today so I haven't had much time to consider it. I promised him though that if you really wanted me to I'd take it on. Well you've made it obvious. I think it is a radical idea, but a good one. There's going to be a lot of work to do to get it rolling, a lot of work. You'll be engaged in that work, every one of you. As long as you promise to do your part I promise to do mine. I thank you all for what you're about to do, for making a start on bringing a civil society into these hard times. I'm assured that this is a legitimate government, but with big problems to solve. Together we'll solve them. Our first great challenge of course is to win this war. We have to continue to make that our number one priority.

I'll say this much more, and then I'll be quiet. I've never seen or been associated with finer men and women than those gathered right here. You are the cream of the crop of Texas citizens. It will be an honor, an absolute honor to serve you in our new government—Long Live The Republic Of Texas!"

It was dawn before the camp was quiet again.

CHAPTER 24

RACE HEARD OF THE RADIO broadcast of the creation of the Republic of Texas from one of the cooks. She was stunned, as she had no idea that Adrian had become involved in creating a new nation.

Race knew immediately that the Rangers were going to Cotulla, but she also knew that if the Admiral thought the girls had that idea in mind they would be held on the ship.

Race gathered the girls and told them what she had learned, "Adrian has been elected the President of the Republic of Texas along with going to war with Mexico."

The girls were as surprised as she had been, their expressions a mixture of shock and puzzlement.

"We have to go to Cotulla and fight with him," Race continued. "But, we can't let anyone know we're going, or they won't let us off the ship. This is extremely important...*Do not let on that we're going to go to war with Adrian.* Swear it now, hold your right hands up and say 'I swear.'"

The girls all immediately did so.

"Good," Race said, satisfied. "I'll tell the Admiral we're going on a training exercise for two days, and that we're going to be just outside Corpus city limits on the north side. We'll head for Cotulla as soon as we're out of sight and drive non-stop. By the time they start looking for us to the north of the city we'll already be in Cotulla."

Six hours after leaving the ship Race pulled the truck off the road and into a thick stand of mesquites.

"We'll spend the night here." She was tired from the driving, the truck's lack of power steering made it a difficult physical activity. Navigation had been simple though. She had an old highway map in the truck and it was a simple matter of taking the highway from Corpus to Cotulla across inhospitable semi-arid country.

The girls dismounted from the truck following their training. They hit the ground in a circle with rifles ready. When they determined that the immediate area was safe, four scouts disappeared into the brush to check out the larger area. While the scouts were out the other girls stretched the circle out to control the perimeter of their camp site, and waited quietly for the scouts' return.

After receiving the all-quiet report from the scouts, sentries were posted further out around the camp. Only then did the camp preparation commence. Wood was gathered, first to resupply the truck's wood gas generator, then for a cooking fire. They made a small meal from some of the canned goods in the truck, and ate quickly. When the dishes were cleaned and all utensils returned to the truck, the girls got their bedrolls and went to sleep. Sleep came fast for most of them.

Race lay awake long into the night, looking up at the stars through the mesquite limbs. She was too tired and too excited to fall asleep straight away. She had wanted to drive straight through to Cotulla, but the truck's top speed on wood gas was only about thirty miles per hour. With the two rest stops they'd taken, they'd averaged twenty miles per hour.

Even so, they were close to Cotulla. She didn't want to get too close just yet, anyway. She knew that Adrian would send them back—and not only would he send them back, but he would assign an escort which would waste resources that he probably couldn't spare. Her plan was to locate Adrian's camp, then watch it until they left and either join up at the last minute or follow along behind.

Race tried to still her mind, force herself to relax. Adrian had instructed her and the Rangers on the value of sleep. *"You never know when danger will strike,"* he had often said. *"When you're in danger, you need to be able to react and to think rapidly. Being tired or sleep-deprived dramatically lowers how fast you can react and how fast you can think. It also lowers your capability to think clearly. Imagine you were on a strong drug when danger approached, it's about the same result as being exhausted. Soldiers learn to sleep wherever they are and whenever they can. They may have to go long hours, sometimes days, without rest when in combat. So they catch what sleep they can whenever they can."*

By the second changing of the sentries she had finally fallen into a restless sleep, one that was dogged by dreams of doubts that she was doing the right thing.

"How long have they been missing? Over." Adrian asked the Admiral.

"Three days. We've had a search party out looking for them since this morning. They weren't going far, just to the north edge of the city. I'm praying nothing has happened to them, Adrian. If you start thinking that you'll come and look for them...don't. I have thirty men out looking and you would add nothing of value to the search. Over."

"Did they know about the war Admiral? Over."

"Maybe. We tried to keep it from them, but you know how people talk. It's possible. What are you thinking? Over."

Adrian paused for a long moment. "I'm thinking they're hiding out near here. They had more than enough time to get here and if they heard about the war I strongly suspect this is where they were headed. If I may suggest, have your men keep looking but have them do it on the west side of town instead. They may find someone that saw the truck headed this way. Meanwhile I'm going to check around the area here, see if I'm right or not. Over."

Adrian called in the scout commander. "Ralph, I have an exercise for you." Adrian explained about the girls and their training. "I want you to locate their camp. I'm pretty sure they're nearby. Focus east of our camp, I suspect they came in on FM 624, and that they have set up near it within a couple of hours walking distance of here."

"When you find them, don't attempt to make contact. These girls are well-trained, and if they think you're a threat, they'll shoot you without hesitation. Just find them and then come back and tell me where they are. And be extremely careful, you'll have to see them first and not be seen at all. Got it?"

"Yes sir. I'll be back as soon as I can."

Ralph was back by noon the next day.

"Found them General, right about where you said. I just waited 'til dark then climbed the nearest microwave tower. Spotted their campfire right off— small, practically smokeless, but you can't hide the glow. You didn't want me to get too close to them or let them know I was around, so I waited until the sun was coming up and climbed the tower again. With binoculars I could tell they were girls, even though they're dressed in camouflage; girls move different than men. These are young girls, sixteen of them from my count."

"Excellent work, Ralph. Show me on the map."

That night, well after dark Adrian walked into the girl's camp. He easily bypassed the sentries because he knew their habits; he knew how many sentries and about where they would be located, making locating them easy enough. Adrian wanted to make a point that they weren't nearly as savvy as they thought they were.

Adrian was sitting down next to the fire almost before the girls realized he was there. They had been staring into the fire and had lost their night vision.

"Damn Race, I just walked right in on you, and making enough noise you should have heard me a mile off. I thought I trained you better than this, staring into a fire at night like that. This is what happens when you get to feeling comfortable and in control, you relax. Don't think I did anything special either, there's probably three hundred people in my camp that could have done it just as easily."

Adrian stirred the fire with a stick while he waited for Race to get her breath.

She and the other girls, had all jumped when he spoke, he had scared them near to death. Adrian had wanted to have the psychological edge and had gained it handily.

Race was shaken, her adrenaline pumping a mile a minute. "Jesus H. Christ Adrian!" she finally stammered out. "We've got loaded guns all over the place and anyone of us could have shot you sneaking in like that."

"You could've if you'd been properly alert, if you hadn't ruined your night vision staring into a fire. Those are amateur mistakes, Race, the kind that can get your crew killed. I've told you, use the fire for cooking and then put it out. A dark camp is a safer camp. Enough of that. What are you doing here?" Adrian asked the last question with a stern tone of voice, a voice that brooked no foolishness.

Race tried to get the advantage back, "We heard on the radio that you, Mr. President of the new Republic of Texas, are going to war with Mexico, and were asking for volunteers. We've come to help. We won't go back, sir, not anyway or anyhow. If you don't let us help, we'll follow you and help anyway." Race spoke with a fierce directness, trying to stare Adrian down. She didn't like it that he had gotten the jump on her. She already knew it would be an uphill battle getting to stay and this didn't help.

"Disobeying orders is not a small infraction," replied Adrian sternly. "You may think you can 'cute' your way out of the consequences, but you can't. I relied on you to follow my orders, Race, and you failed me. I am bitterly disappointed."

Adrian continued, looking at all of the girls as he spoke. "You have caused me to lose valuable time in training and organizing for the upcoming battle. That lack of attention may very well cause people to die, people that, if they had that extra attention, might have lived. What you have done in your arrogance and flagrant disregard for the trust I put in you has serious and probably fatal consequences to other people. Not to mention that you have clearly demonstrated that my trust was misplaced." Adrian's voice was like ice.

Race was shocked to her core, he had never spoken to her like that and it was a side of him she hadn't suspected. She realized as each icy word pierced her heart that Adrian was telling the truth, telling it like it was, and that he was right.

"I'm sorry Adrian, I...I didn't think of any of that. We just wanted to help."

"No Race, you don't get off that easy, I'm not buying that. If you had wanted to help, you would have followed orders, honored our agreement. You've gotten a big head, placed your ego above the safety of these girls that follow you out of loyalty. When you needlessly and recklessly endanger your troops, you aren't fit for command. What you wanted was a share in what you think is the glory of battle, to win approval and to be respected. This is all about foolish ego, like Custer's was."

Race was crestfallen. She felt like crying, but with a huge effort stifled the tears. She waited for more of the dressing down that she now realized she deserved. She knew that she would be taking the Rangers back to the ship in the morning.

"Adrian, please...I was wrong. Worse than wrong, I was stupid and you're right, I wanted to be in the battle. I'll...I'll take the girls back tomorrow at first light." In spite of her best efforts she felt hot tears scalding her face. She looked down, hoping to hide them.

"No. I obviously can't trust you to do what you'll say." With this Race's heart broke in half and she openly wept.

Adrian watched her for a long moment, then continued. "I would have to send a team with you to make sure you got there, and even then I couldn't trust you not to sneak off the ship again somehow—you've demonstrated a remarkable ability for getting on and off that ship at will. I need those people here to continue training, they need every minute of training they can get, I've already explained why."

"So you leave me no choice but to take you into camp with me. And don't for a minute think you're going to enjoy being there. You girls will be placed under camp arrest and you'll be assigned to kitchen duty. You'll scrape and wash every dirty dish in that camp from daylight to dark, then you'll wash clothes until bedtime. You'll be working hard every waking minute of your day. And understand this completely: when it comes time to fight, *you will not be part of it.* I would ask you if you understand, but I don't care right now if you do or not, you'll do as your told, period."

Adrian watched her again for a minute. He could see a little of the light coming back into her eyes. He knew that she would do as told this time and was relieved not to be returning to the ship.

Adrian continued, in a milder tone than before, but not a friendly one, "You have a long way to go to earn my trust again, a long way. One slip, one mistake, one disobeyed order and that trust will be gone forever with no getting it back, not ever. Now...do you understand that? Have I communicated clearly?"

Race answered meekly, her expression deadpan, "Yes sir, I understand clearly and won't let you down again, I promise."

She would keep that promise, she knew that for a fact, but she was beginning to smile inside. She was at least going to be near the battle, she and the Rangers would be working hard at menial tasks, but still tasks that supported the war. So they wouldn't be going into battle in a blazing fury as she had daydreamed, but they would be doing their part. And she would earn his trust again, or die trying.

And she would damn sure try to find a way to get Adrian to let the Rangers fight, too.

CHAPTER 25

THE FORT BRAZOS MILITIA ARRIVED the next morning in a convoy of pickup trucks.

When Adrian received the outlying sentry's report, he rushed to the overpass and waited for ten minutes, nervously pacing back and forth, trying to calm himself.

As the first truck came to a stop the driver's door flew open and Linda came rushing out, straight into his arms. Adrian was only dimly aware of the hooting and hollering from the other men in the camp. He was in bliss, holding Linda as tight as he could without cutting off her breath. They embraced for what seemed an eternity. Then they kissed. A long, gentle, soul-satisfying kiss. At this the crowd that had gathered around them roared with delight, but neither Adrian or Linda heard even a whisper.

When they finally released each other they became aware of the crowd around them. Linda blushed, but Adrian just grinned and said loudly, "Anyone ever see a more beautiful woman?"

The crowd roared back at him with approval. Linda turned a deep crimson, but smiled as she looked around at these rough hard men and women that were, in contrast to their looks, obviously romantics at heart.

Adrian took Linda's hand and led her away. The men and women in the crowd didn't follow out of common courtesy, but instead swooped down on Roman, Matt, Perry, Tim, and the rest of the militia with a huge welcome of bear hugs and back slaps. They had all heard of Fort Brazos' war with Rex and were more than delighted to have a trained and recently battle tested group of more Texans joining in the fight.

Adrian said, "Saw the bullet holes in the first three trucks; must have been worse than you told me?"

"Bad enough. We lost two straight up and another from wounds. Several walking injured and one seriously that will make it eventually. Cost us a solid week to tend our wounded and repair the trucks. We'll need to make some arrangement for Ted; he can't go any further, he needs a lot of time to recover. After that, I decided we needed to stop and scout any likely ambush spot long before the convoy got to it. That was a slow process, but your army buddies did a great job. Found two more ambushes that we had to take out. Knowing where they were, we were able to come up with a plan for each one, cleaned them all out without taking more than two more injuries. It's been a rough trip, Adrian; took us two solid weeks to get here," She ran a hand through her hair. "Back in the day we could've been here in ten hours instead of fourteen days."

"I'm just glad you got here safe, you can't imagine how much I worried."

Adrian wrapped his arm tighter around her. "We'll find someone in Cotulla to look after Ted, pick him up again on the way home eventually, don't worry about that anymore."

After another long hug and a longer kiss, Adrian took Linda into the camp to meet the Angels. "Race, bring the girls over. I have someone I want you to meet."

Race quickly gathered the girls from their various kitchen chores. "Linda, this is Race and the Angels. Girls this is Linda."

Race looked at Linda with a touch of awe in her face. "You're beautiful! I knew you would be but...Wow!"

Linda blushed again. "Thank you. I've heard so much about you girls that I almost feel like I already know you. I've never seen tougher-looking girls, yet you're each so gorgeous." This was met with smiles from several dirt-smudged faces.

Race said, "Adrian, I approve. You can marry her."

Adrian at first frowned, but relented with a small grin. "I'm happy to have your approval and permission." He said with no small amount of irony in his voice.

The girls and Linda laughed at this. Everyone was staring at Adrian. He suddenly felt like a piece of meat on an auction block. He had been more comfortable up on the speaking platform being elected President than he was now, and he had been far from comfortable then.

"Uh...I just wanted to introduce you all. Now I need to talk to Linda for a while. If you girls will excuse us?" The two of them walked well away from the camp.

"They are utterly charming Adrian," said Linda, "if

a bit rough around the edges. But what in hell are they doing here?"

"Long story darling. The short version is they went AWOL from the ship and came to get in the battle. I don't dare send them back, they'll just escape and come back. I'm in a pickle with them, can't have them here and can't send them off. Once you get to know them a little you'll understand. They are pretty girls, but God help anyone that crosses them, they are as rough as cobs. I may have made a mistake training them."

"Mistake?" Linda shook her head. "No, I don't think so. If you've trained them to take care of themselves that's not a mistake. A mistake would be to assume they are mature enough to be independent of adult supervision, and since you're keeping them here to keep an eye on them you're not making a mistake there either. The trick will be to keep them safe and away from the fight."

"I've been pondering on that and have an idea, but it's only half-baked right now. I'll get your advice on it when I've given it more thought. But enough of that, what about you and Scott? How have you been? Tell me everything."

They talked for hours, catching up on their time apart and finally came back to the present.

Adrian took both of Linda's hands in his and pulled her to her feet, he got down on one knee and said, "This is probably the worst time in the world to ask this, but our tomorrows aren't guaranteed. Either or both of us might be dead in a couple of weeks and I don't want to go to my grave without asking you formally. Will you Linda Fremont, beautiful wild woman that you are, strong and independent, healthy and young and knowing you can have the pick of any man, will you marry me?"

Linda grasped his hand tightly and pulled until he stood looking down at her. She looked up into his eyes, her vision blurred with tears. "Yes Adrian Hunter, I will marry you. If I had the pick of every man on earth there is no way I would choose any other, not ever, not for as long as I live."

As soon as she stopped talking, a little girl's war whoop broke out from the nearby brush. Startled they both turned to watch as Rita ran off whooping and shouting the news. "They're getting married! They're getting married!"

Before they got back to the camp the news had spread and a huge and wild welcome was waiting for them. As they approached the camp and saw the celebrating and waiting crowd, Adrian said, "Still the girls are charming?"

When they were within shouting distance the crowd started shouting approval. When they were close enough to be heard Adrian raised his hand asking for silence. "Let me be the *second* to inform you that Linda Fremont has graciously accepted my proposal of marriage. May I introduce to you the future First Lady of Texas, Linda Fremont!" Adrian turned and bowed to Linda with a huge smile. As the crowd shouted encouragingly over his announcement, he mouthed the words to her "Bet you didn't think of that!"

Linda leaned close and shouted in Adrian's ear "Of course I did silly, why do you think I accepted?" She then winked at him and kissed him again in front of God and the Republic of Texas Army.

Later that evening, Adrian and Linda were in the Headquarters tent talking to Jose and Ryan.

"No, we haven't set the date yet," said Adrian. "It's not the right time for a honeymoon with a big battle coming up. On the other hand, either of us might not be alive afterwards, so we're in something of a quandry here."

Lind added, "Plus can you imagine us trying to have a honeymoon in this camp? My God, we'd be pestered to death and there's no way I can take to a wedding bed knowing everyone out there is watching our tent. No way."

"I have a suggestion." Jose said. "Get married tomorrow and leave for two days, then come back and get back to work. Adrian, you owe it to Linda to go into that battle married, no matter the outcome. It would be tragic if you don't. We'll carry on with the training without you for that long. I promise if anything dire comes about I'll come and get you right away. Just take one of the trucks and go far enough that you feel alone—let me know where you are—and have two days to yourselves. If you don't I don't know if these men and women will go nuts, but I think the tension just might drive them crazy. It will be the best thing for you two, and best for the camp, too. Just expect a large wedding party and a big send off. Oh, and probably a lot of winks and nods when you get back." Jose finished with a smile.

Adrian turned to Linda and said, "I like it. What do you think?"

Her smile was answer enough.

To Adrian's dismay, most of the training activity came to a halt in order to prepare for the wedding. Adrian barely caught site of Linda once that day. And he was busier than he'd had any thought of. Ryan had scoured the camp for a suit for him to wear, a tough challenge given the nature of the camp and Adrian's size. But with the help of two seamstresses and a lot of standing for Adrian to be measured and fitted, the ladies turned the pieces Ryan had found into a tux that would be presentable almost anywhere.

Linda was in a whirl of activity. The ladies flocked to her to help her put a wedding dress together and to make dresses for Adrian's Angels who would act as bride's maids. A group of carpenters constructed a large arbor for them to stand under and other volunteers decorated it profusely, including the new Republic of Texas flags. All was ready an hour before dark.

Adrian stood in the arbor and watched as the girls came out of the bride's tent. He was startled, having seen them only in rags and uniforms. The girls were washed and clean with shiny hair and bright faces, all wearing pretty dresses. He couldn't help smiling broadly at them, and they smiled shyly back, not used to being dressed in such feminine attire and having the added distraction of a large crowd clapping and whistling at them.

Adrian had never seen their faces so pink, nor so happy.

As three guitars played the wedding march, Adrian waited nervously, it was all he could do not to fidget. But he forgot his nervousness when Linda appeared. Somehow the ladies had put together a modestly-cut wedding dress of white lace that still managed to show her figure to advantage.

As she came closer, Adrian's nervousness returned. He lifted her veil and beamed back at the full smile she gave him. "You're beyond beautiful," he said. "You're like an angel come to earth."

Taking her hand they both turned to face Matt, the Fort Brazos Church Pastor and Adrian's dear friend. Adrian held her hand and couldn't tell which one of them was trembling the most.

"Dearly beloved..." Matt began. Matt's deep baritone voice carried over the crowd effortlessly. Many of the women and even some of the men had tears.

When the ceremony was over and they were finally able to disengage from the party afterwards, Adrian and Linda slipped away in a truck and drove the few miles to their honeymoon location. Ryan and Jose had set up a tent for them, packed it with plenty of food that didn't need to be cooked and even a bottle of wine they had scrounged. Inside the tent was a table holding the food and wine and a large bed, complete with frame, box springs and a new mattress that someone had found in a furniture store in Cotulla.

Upon inspection Adrian said "Maybe I ought to drag that bed outside. I'm afraid we might set the tent on fire."

Linda laughed, "Maybe?" she replied, in a tone of voice that assured they would indeed.

They had two days alone before they returned to the war preparations, and they made the most of it.

CHAPTER 26

ADRIAN BRIEFED THE COMMANDERS. "IT'S time to take the show on the road, gentlemen. The Mexicans are four days from the river. Our train is ready, the fuel tankers, assault trucks, and transport trucks are all loaded, the tracks have been cleared of obstructions. Our troops are trained as well as they're going to be given our timeline. I'm damned impressed at how fast they get into position from a standing start, and how well they execute their assignments. Spread the word to pack up, we leave at midnight."

At dawn two days later, Adrian was looking over the battle zone. The cartel's army would be planning to cross the Rio Grande at Hwy 277, the only bridge for miles in either direction. Once they realized the bridge was denied to them, they would look for another place to cross. Adrian looked to his right at the big canal on the US side. Crossing there would present the enemy with two water crossings. To his left, and across the river on the Mexican side, was a large sports complex, an open area of soccer and football fields that begged to be used to mass the troops for a surge across the river. *That's where they'll cross, and that's where we'll be waiting.*

Adrian turned and walked back and then along

the river's edge opposite the sports compound. The river was narrow here and the water was low, affording a relatively easy crossing. Their command trucks wouldn't make it across, but Adrian knew the Mexicans would simply abandon them, expecting to get more trucks on the US side.

On his own side, there were scattered trees on this side, enough to keep his troops out of sight, not enough to give the enemy troops much cover. It was about as good as he could have hoped for; his scouts had reported the area accurately. His planned tactics had taken all of this into account.

Returning to the command post half a mile from the river Adrian began issuing orders. "Take Company D across the river after dark. They'll then move east along the river's frontage road four miles and hide. We blow the middle section of the bridge as soon as they cross. Did you find enough ammonium nitrate fertilizer to blow it, Frank?"

"Yes sir, more than enough. It's loaded onto a trailer already. We'll just tow the trailer out there and put the diesel fuel into it, then four sticks of dynamite as an igniter. We'll also place ANFO charges at the base of the support columns beneath the charge, they'll be wired together and all go off at the same time."

"Excellent, but just in case it doesn't do enough damage what's your plan B"?

"Do it again. We brought up reserve supplies of material and can set off a second blast within a half hour sir."

"Good. Groups A, B and C, will take position just after dark and wait. No fires, no movement of any kind. I expect them to send scouts across the river as soon as they see the blown bridge. I'm not sure how far their scouts will go. They may get close enough to spot us; if, and only if, they do spot us, the Seals will take them out with silent weapons. Otherwise we want them to go back and give an all clear, to report that that this is the best place to cross."

"Even if they do spot us, I think they'll still come across here. They don't know what our tactics will be, they'll probably expect a simple heads-on clash, one they can win by sheer numbers. Moving up or down the river to cross somewhere else won't appeal to them, knowing that we'll simply move along with them. My guess is that they'll cross about noon tomorrow, they'll find the blown bridge shortly after daylight, then they'll need time to send scouts, make their decision and get their men into position."

He looked at his men. "You've trained for this. You know what you're supposed to do and when. I have complete, no, I have *absolute* faith that you'll do your jobs, and complete your missions with total success. By sundown tomorrow this will be over, and I am fully confident we will win. Take your positions as soon as it's dark and don't forget to have your Chaplains' move among your troops giving prayers in small groups. Wait for my signal tomorrow. I'll radio it to you. The word to move out is 'execute.' Any questions?"

Adrian didn't expect any questions, they had gone over this a hundred times, practiced it until the only challenge became one of beating their previous best time.

There were no questions.

"Dismissed, and God be with you."

Adrian watched as the cartel's forward scouts approached the bridge and spotted the missing segment in the middle. The first round of explosives had dropped the section straight down into the river. The scouts stared at it for a few minutes, talking to each other and waving their hands. They turned and double-timed back the way they had come.

He turned to Linda who was standing next to him. As a full Colonel, Linda was commanding the Fort Brazos Militia. Adrian knew and trusted these men and women and wanted them in Group B.

"It's a shame we had to give them this forewarning, but letting them across the bridge would have strung them out in too long of a line, and it would be a line that kept moving."

"I can't think of any flaws in your plan Adrian. But as you said, the best plan can go out the window with the first hit."

"I've seen that time and again, that's why we have two backup plans. Both can work but have some iffy points in them. Either of them depends entirely on timing, and we didn't have a lot of time to practice them as much as I would have liked. Still, we have some nasty surprises for those bastards."

"I know you really hate having to stay behind the lines and direct troop movements. My hunch is that you'd far rather be leading one of the front line companies."

Adrian waited a minute before replying as he scanned the bridge again through the binoculars.

"Yes, I would much rather be out front. I've never had to stay back and direct the overall battle, and it's frustrating as hell to send troops into battle instead of leading them in myself."

"You know as well as I do it has to be this way. No one out there would trust anyone but you to call the shots, directing them to be where the need is greatest. They admire you, Adrian, flat out love you in fact. If you went down in the battle they would lose heart and possibly lose because of it. They all know you would rather be in front of them—they know that, Adrian. The fact is that you have to force yourself to stay back...they know you have to and not only want it that way but love you for doing it. They are well aware that you are doing it for their sakes. Look! The main body is coming down the road now. Jesus Christ! Would you look at how many there are."

Adrian watched as the much larger than expected column of men paused short of the bridge, then moved towards the sports complex. He saw eight scouts cross the river on each side of the bridge to check the terrain. It was a tense two hours, listening for any shouts or gunfire from the scouts, hoping against hope they were too lazy to go far enough to spot the Texas troops. Four scouts returned from the right side, the side Adrian didn't want the Mexicans to cross. It was another hour before the scouts on the left side returned.

Adrian picked up the radio and called his forward observers. "Did they spot anyone? Over."

"No sir." Came the quiet reply. "They crossed over, came in about three hundred yards and sat down to eat. Then they crossed back. Over."

"Acknowledged." Adrian said just as quietly.

Linda said, "It's time for me to join our Militia, Adrian. Please, please stay here. We desperately need you to have clear sight of the battle and to direct troops as needed. Promise me you'll stay."

Adrian desperately wanted to keep Linda with him, but knew she wouldn't. Couldn't. He gave her a long kiss. "Be safe," he said, pushing a stray lock of hair out of her face. "And come back to me unharmed."

Linda touched his face, her hand resting there for just a moment, then turned and walked away.

Adrian watched with a sadness he couldn't give words to as she disappeared down the hill side. Immediately after Linda was out of sight the girls came closer to him. They each had binoculars and would assist Adrian in watching from the row of foxholes at the top of the hill, and would report to him anything he needed to know about. It was the best he could think of to keep them out of harm's way, and to make them useful as well. Bear was at his side, seeming to know the import of the moment. A long hour later he watched as the cartel army began crossing the river.

They came across in a wide column, looking like a huge army of ants from Adrian's vantage point. They muddied the water, the brown silt stirred by the thousands of feet staining the river as it flowed downstream. It took them over half an hour to complete the crossing and move up the bank on to the Texas side of the border four hundred yards before stopping again, just as Adrian had hoped they would. They had crossed barefooted and would need time to put on their dry socks and boots, get organized for the next move.

As soon as the last wave was across, Adrian picked up his radio, "Ground One to Air One, hit them hard. And remember, our troops are close by in position, as previously described. Over."

"Air One to Ground One, we'll be overhead in three minutes. We'll be careful of your position Ground One, no worry there. Out."

Two minutes later Adrian could hear the faint rumbling of the four F-16's approach. As predicted at the third minute the first jet roared as it came in low and slow. Adrian watched the cartel army looking up with panic-stricken faces. Some of them shouldered rifles and began firing at the jet. He saw the F-16 release the cluster bombs and watched as they popped open in mid-air scattering the small bomblets. Explosions ripped through the cartel's ranks, fire balls erupting in a long trail that started at the front line of the Mexicans and extended to the river. Men's bodies cartwheeled through the air. Just as the explosions ended but before all the bodies had fallen, the next jet was coming in and releasing its bombs. Adrian watched and this time he didn't see anyone firing at the jet, instead they were desperately seeking cover, any cover.

Adrian spoke into the battle communications radio, "Execute, Execute, Execute!"

The three groups of combined companies began wheeling into position, all of them on trucks. Group A was lining up directly in front of the enemy in a broad line. As the trucks wheeled into position the troops dismounted and spread into a line. Group B did the same on the left front and Group C on the right, along highway 277. Timing was critical, Adrian didn't want his troops to be too close when the next two jets dropped their bombs, but he didn't want them to get there too late to contain the panicked cartel army.

Jet Three screamed in and dropped more bombs, timed perfectly to begin erupting just seconds after the previous explosions. Then the fourth and final jet came in, this time dropping napalm. Adrian watched calmly as he watched the fire storm of jellied gasoline spread over the enemy troops. He didn't envy anyone that kind of pain and death, but it was effective and effective was what counted. The fire had the added benefit of stripping away the brush and trees limbs that hid some of the men, not only killing but also clearing the field for better vision for what was to come. As the flames died down a little, Adrian saw his troops moving in on the three sides, boxing the enemy in with the river to their back. He watched a flawless execution, the Texans rapidly moving into place and spreading out at the right distances from each other, firing immediately into the shocked and confused enemy ranks.

The Mexicans were better disciplined than he had hoped for; in spite of the pounding from the air, they were quickly moving into battle formations. He saw men dropping rapidly as the Texan's rifle fire poured into them, but still they formed into a solid group and began moving towards Group A in an attempt to break out of the box. As they moved forward, the Texans closest to the river began moving forward as well, leaving the river open behind the Mexicans. This was part of the plan: to move and flow with the enemy, but to leave them the inviting aspect of crossing back over.

Right on schedule, Adrian saw Group D, the river boat trucks moving into hidden positions across the river. *Excellent, just as they were supposed to. The final surprise.*

CHAPTER 27

ADRIAN CONTINUED TO WATCH AND listen to the radio as each company called in and moved, describing their position. He had wished for more air cover, but the round trip back to the carrier to reload was too long, and would give the enemy too much time to regroup. It was all up to the ground pounders now.

The Mexicans were taking steady and deadly fire from the Texans, Mexicans falling by the scores. He saw Texans falling as well, and saw the medical corpsmen rush to their aid, placing them on stretchers and moving them back to the field hospital using pickup trucks as ambulances. The Mexicans either couldn't give aid to their wounded under the intense fire being poured into them.

With a discipline that Adrian found admirable, the Mexicans continued to pull into formation and move towards the front line, and there were still too many of them, way too many. Adrian, never one to underestimate an enemy was ready for this. He called on his radio "Bear to Mobile One, move into position with Group A, reserve four trucks for Groups B and C. Over."

"Mobile One to Bear, moving out now. Out."

Before the trucks could get there, a group of twenty

or so Mexicans broke through the line and came straight at the hill Adrian and the girls were on. The Texans quickly closed the gap in a fierce, blistering fight, holding the rest of the Mexicans in the box. Adrian watched the Mexican group, expecting them to turn and fire at the Texans from the rear, but they didn't, they hauled ass as fast as they could, still heading straight towards Adrian's hill.

"Stay down!"Adrian commanded. The girls did as told, keeping their heads low as they put down their binoculars and pointed their rifles down the hill at the oncoming Mexicans who had apparently spotted them. Adrian hoped they would deflect off, but having seen what was happening to their comrades they appeared to be on a mission to cut off the snakes head, as they still came straight at the hill. Adrian remained standing where he could see the battle better.

One of the approaching Mexicans stopped to aim and fire, the bullet making a sonic crack as it went by Adrian's head. The girls in the foxholes immediately began to return fire. Several of the attackers fell, the rest diving for cover. Adrian knew he should take cover, but he needed to see the battle clearly so he remained standing.

"Rangers! Keep the fire on them hot and heavy, I want their heads down so I can stay up and see the battle." The girls immediately began firing more rapidly and Adrian could see where the bullets were hitting all around where the men had taken cover.

Within two minutes Adrian observed the armored pickup trucks armed with chain guns moving into the front line of Group A. The driver jumped out and took position in the back of the truck with the gunner to assist with ammunition feeding and also shooting enemy combatants with his rifle. The chain guns operated by an electric motor and could be fired at variable speeds of up to 570 rounds per minute. Adrian had elected to have them fire at a lower rate to give more control and to make the ammunition last longer. Each chain gun was equivalent, even at the lower rate of fire, to two hundred rifles being fired once per minute. They were also extremely frightening to face. Even at the lower speeds the tracers, one in every ten rounds, looked like a solid stream of fire, making targeting easy and intuitive for the gunner.

As the chain guns began firing into the enemy front lines, the number of bodies dropping increased dramatically. Within another minute, the two chain guns assigned to Groups B and C began firing into the enemy also. Between the infantry fire and the chain guns, the enemy's position quickly became untenable; no matter how much discipline and drive they had, the rate of bullets flying into their packed mass was mowing them down at a phenomenal rate.

The Mexicans withstood the barrage from three sides for only two more minutes, then a general rout began developing along the back of their lines. They were faced with almost certain death if they continued or a chance to escape back across the river.

When Adrian saw the first group of men take off toward the river, he spoke into the radio, "Bear to Mobile One. Increase rate of fire on chain guns, go to maximum now!"

The chain guns all momentarily stopped firing as the gunners reset the motor speed to go to maximum firing speed, effectively tripling the rate of fire. Then they started firing again and the bodies dropped at a faster rate than before. *That will encourage the retreat.* And indeed it did. With a herd instinct, the remains of the cartel's army turned and fled towards the river. Still taking intense fire they stumbled and fell over the fallen bodies, tripped over rocks and roots, scrambled to their feet and took off running again.

Adrian called into the radio "Group D take position and fire at will. Groups A, B, and C move forward as fast as they retreat. "

He watched as the relayed message went through. The infantry started chasing after the retreating army, steadily pouring bullets into them. The chain gun trucks became mobile again, chain gun firing steadily as the truck advanced apace with the ground troops. Groups B and C began flowing towards the river, maintaining fire from the sides with deadly effect and keeping the routed army from trying to escape to either side. The Mexicans were herded into the river. Group D had pulled their trucks up to the river's edge and as the Mexicans began entering the water poured deadly chain fire into them.

When the bulk of the Mexicans were in the river, Groups A, B, and C followed them to the river's edge, continuing to fire into the fleeing mass of men. The carnage was absolutely brutal, men being hit and trampled as thousands of rounds a minute poured into them from both sides. Chain guns from Groups C and D cut them down along the outside edges of the fleeing troops, preventing them from escaping up or down river. The river flowed a dirty red from the blood pouring out of the now hundreds of injured bodies and the silt disturbed they their feet.

It took only three minutes once they were in the river. Minutes of continual fire from the Texans and only the occasional shot back at them as the men in the river knew their death was only seconds away and fired back more out of anger than any hope of being effective. Three long, horrifying minutes and then the firing came to a sputtering stop. The silence was incredible. It lasted a full minute, Adrian, even from where he was, could hear the wild jubilant shouting of the Texans.

He also noted that there was still a group of Mexicans creeping slowly up his hill.

Adrian now could take cover with the girls and got into the foxhole with Race. He told her, "They're going to run or surrender or attack when we stop firing. Could go either way. They know there's only enemy behind them now, so they're deciding to try to get away or surrender or commit suicide. Tell the girls to cease fire but remain ready. We'll give them a chance to surrender."

When the girls stopped firing, the men below waited a moment, then they all stood and charged the hill firing as fast as they could. There were still over a dozen of them and they came running into the teeth of death with no real hope of surviving. Adrian yelled out, "Pick your targets and make every shot count!" Immediately the girls and Adrian began firing, and the Mexican men charging at them began falling. The last one died within feet of the foxholes.

Adrian called the girls out of their positions and Race got them into formation. "Rangers" Adrian said, "If you hadn't been here I would be dead now. You have saved my life and I deeply appreciate it. Race, you've earned my trust again, fully. Now let's get down to the battlefield and help our wounded."

"How many men and women did we lose?" It was Adrian's first question to the assembled commanders.

"One hundred and thirty three dead, three hundred and twelve wounded." came the reply.

Adrian sat somberly for a few moments. "Nearly a quarter of our troops." He paused for a few seconds and asked "Enemy casualties?"

"We're estimating at this point sir, but it looks like over four thousand dead or critically wounded and about five hundred wounded that might survive. We're giving them medical treatment as fast as we can, after we took care of our own first, but we're giving them the best treatment we can. We have nearly five hundred prisoners. We think about two hundred escaped across the river."

Adrian had issued orders that the Texans were not to deliberately fire on any clearly unarmed combatants trying to escape once they were in the river. That order had three reasons. To not place the Texans into a position of being mere executioners, to allow escape so that word of the disastrous results of the attempted invasion would spread far and rapidly, and to prevent as much as possible for any of the Texans to have doubts about the carnage they would wreak on the enemy. It was far from a perfect solution, but it was the best that could be done in the heat of battle and to assure victory as well.

"You are all to be congratulated, you executed beautifully, flawlessly," Adrian said. "You have won a great battle, one where you were severely outnumbered. By a combination of the element of surprise, superior fire power, pure guts and perfect execution, you and all of our troops have destroyed this enemy for years to come. One of the first actions of the new government will be to recognize all of our fallen, wounded, and unwounded. Medals will be created and I will personally place those medals on every single person as soon as possible."

"We need to immediately locate a superior burial ground for our fallen and get them interred with respect and dignity. And we need to send the fallen enemy troops back to their people. They deserve proper burial in their own homeland. Strip their bodies of arms and ammunition, and have the prisoners carry the bodies across the river and lay them out in the sports complex. See to it immediately after our own have been properly buried. No, get a contingent started on it right away, but give them leave to attend the funeral services for our own, then have them get right back to work."

"As soon as those duties are attended to we'll board the train and return to Cotulla where we'll have a final ceremony and disburse. Any questions? No? Dismissed."

Two days later, Adrian spoke to the assembled Texas army at the memorial service.

"We are saddened beyond measure that these men and women are dead. They came here to fight, believing in something greater than themselves. They put their lives on the line for that belief. They believed, and rightly so, that the time had come for Texas to resurrect itself, to create a place in this world where men and women and children can expect to be treated with dignity. A place where law and order would offer them as much protection as it's possible for a civilized society to grant. They believed, as we all do, that if the invasion had been successful all Texans would suffer enormously, that this deadly peril had to be stopped right here and right now."

"They have given their lives, a gift that can't be bought or borrowed but only freely granted. The ultimate of all gifts, the gift of absolute love. These men and women whose names we called a moment ago, shall be remembered throughout the span of time that the Republic of Texas exists. They will be honored every year on the day of their death as the first men and women of Texas. By official decree, this day shall be considered holy...in their honor. We'll call it the Battle of the Del Rio Day. On that day each year their names will be read out by the President of the Republic of Texas in an official and public display to honor their greatest gift of all."

"Reverend Matthew will lead us all in prayer, followed by the playing of Taps and the lowering of the Republic of Texas Flag to half-staff, where it will remain for one full year in honor of our fallen. Not until the first anniversary of the battle will the flag be lifted again to full staff, again in their honor. We will be reminded every time we see the flag flying that it was because of their greatest sacrifice and the great sacrifices of the wounded and unwounded that came to this place to keep Texans free. Reverend, if you please."

Linda reached up with her hand and gently wiped the tears from his face.

CHAPTER 28

THEY RETURNED TO COTULLA A week later, after giving the Mexican soldiers what honors they could. Only a very few people came to claim bodies or try to.

Adrian had ordered a bull dozer to be repaired and sent to the Mexican side of the river to dig long trenches six feet deep. The Mexican prisoners carefully and respectfully placed the bodies in the trenches and then covered by hand with shovels; everyone agreed that pushing the dirt in with the bulldozer seemed disrespectful.

Every uninjured person turned out to help with the laying out of the bodies and covering them, along with the prisoners. A large steel cross was mounted above the burial site, permanently embedded in concrete, matching the monument at the Texas side. Adrian had ordered the two crosses be exactly the same. Unknown to him though, the welders had made the Texas cross a foot longer in each dimension. A flag pole was erected and a Mexican flag flown at half-mast.

A Catholic priest, among the Texans, led the main prayer; a second prayer for Protestants that might be in the group was also said by Matt. After the final memorial ceremony, Adrian released the

Mexican prisoners, then the Texas army loaded up on the train and returned to Cotulla.

In Cotulla, the camp was temporarily restored. Many of the men and women left for home immediately, but the elected representatives stayed, there was still a government to finish building. There were also wounded to tend to before they would be able to return home.

For two months, the elected officials worked at crafting the new Constitution and the structural make-up of the government. It was different in several critical ways from the former Constitution of the United States. They were busy days, filled with the excitement and the promise of creating something larger than the men and women at work on it. They were heady days that were filled with debates starting at daylight and continuing until deep into the night. Slowly, but surely, the articles of the Constitution took form and shape and were agreed on.

Perry headed the Constitutional convention. In the pre-grid days he had been a lawyer with a penchant for a libertarian style of government. The basic premise of his draft Constitution was that every individual was a sovereign unto himself, and that the government wasn't there to override or to rule him, but to create an environment where each person could live his or her life in accordance with their own beliefs, and so far as the actions of these persons did not infringe on the rights of others to be left alone to live as they saw fit.

Building on this premise, it was determined that the Republic of Texas would be a volunteer republic;

it would disallow elected officials to gain any compensation for their position in any way. They would be paid no salary; they would not be able to gain by any form of business dealing while in office or after being in office that relied even partially on granting favors or giving untoward access to their voting, or inside knowledge. In effect, there would be no special interest lobbying or buying of favors.

The new republic's government would rely on funding to support its activities not by taxes, but by fees on international trade and by voluntary gifts from citizens. There would be no standing army, but all interested citizens of eighteen years or more could be militia members, with each section of the state creating its own militia. Voting would be restricted to those that served in the militia or had served previously in the militia and left it with honor. The general consensus was that voting would not be an automatic right, but a right that could be earned by one and all, if they so chose to.

Each militia would patrol its section of the Republic. The militia would provide the hammer and the constitution would provide the anvil to crush those that acted outside the common consent of law. The justice system would act much as it had in the pre-grid days, all crimes except of a minor offense, would require indictment by a grand jury, representation of the accused by competent counsel, and a trial by jury. However, there would be no jails, there would be no prison terms. If the accused were found guilty of an offense serious enough to have received prison time in the previous world, they would be expelled from the republic on threat of death if they attempted to return. Capital offenders, if found guilty, would be executed after an expedited re-trial and upon unanimous vote by the second jury.

It was a rough-and-ready form of government, but one suited to the times.

Even after the new government was complete and the injured healed enough to go home on their own, or to be taken home by volunteers, there was still much to be done. Adrian and Linda had barely gotten back home to Fort Brazos, the capital of the new republic, when a helicopter appeared over the village.

Adrian and Linda came out on the porch at the sound of the hovering craft and watched it land gently in the open field in front of their new home, built for them by the villagers between the victory and Adrian's return with Linda. It was a large, log structure, with a huge living room suitable for greeting official visitors and holding meetings of up to twenty people comfortably. It was a fitting symbol of the new republic: rustically elegant, setting an example that government structures should be simple and have multiple uses. The Republic flag was flying in front of the house, at half-mast.

They watched as the Admiral dismounted from the helicopter, quickly followed by Ryan, Jose, and another man in Navy uniform that Adrian didn't recognize. Adrian greeted the men with a firm handshake and large smile for each, as did Linda who quickly followed suit.

"Welcome to our home gentlemen, it's good to see all of you again." A crowd was quickly forming out of curiosity at the helicopter's arrival. "Admiral," Adrian continued, "if we don't satisfy their curiosity as to who you are and why you're here they'll be making up rumors of another impending invasion."

The Admiral smiled and shook his head. "Just some business that needs tending to."

"Well Admiral, since I don't know what that business is, why don't you say a few words to the crowd and then we'll go inside and talk."

The Admiral nodded and turned to the crowd, speaking to them from the raised porch. "Ladies and Gentlemen, I know you're curious about my loud arrival, and I don't blame you a bit. It's simply that I'm here to discuss government business with the President, just routine business, nothing exciting or all that interesting. I'm sure that President Hunter, or should I call him President Bear as most people do, will make a full announcement after I leave. I believe in transparency in government as much as he does, so come back after I leave to get the details." He smiled and waved and the crowd began slowly dispersing.

"Tit for tat Adrian—you threw me under the bus, so I returned the favor." The Admiral said in a jovial tone of voice. "Now, how about some of that famous Texas hospitality?"

As they seated themselves at the dinner table, the Admiral said, "Let me introduce Jeff Parsons. He is, it turns out, an economist by avocation. He has a doctorate in the subject and wrote many papers that were well-received in the old days. His choice to be a Naval officer instead of a civilian economist comes from the desire for adventure and a life at sea. We've had many talks on economics, a subject I also find fascinating, although as a layman, and we've been discussing the future of Texas. Let me turn it over to him now."

"Thank you Admiral," said Jeff. "It's an honor and a privilege to meet you Mr. President."

Adrian stopped him with a raised hand. "Jeff, there may be official times to call me by that title, but not in my home. Here you will do me the honor of calling me Adrian, if you please. If not then we'll have to go somewhere else to talk." Adrian punctuated that sentence with a big smile.

Jeff replied, "Thank you sir, I mean...thank you, Adrian." He was clearly uncomfortable addressing him informally.

"I am an economist as the Admiral has stated, and as he said we've had many interesting conversations about the new republic and how it will handle economic matters. I have some ideas that I'd like to bounce off you, if you have the time to allow me to."

Adrian turned to Linda "Do we have anything pressing today? I can't think of anything can you?"

"Nothing official, and nothing that can't wait. We were going to visit the girls later, but we can do that after this." Linda replied.

"The floor is yours Jeff, but be advised...don't get jargonish on me or you'll lose me."

"Yes sir... I mean, Adrian...this is all basic stuff but if I start to wax unintelligible just stop me. What it boils down to is that every nation has to have some form of currency, some form of officially recognized money system. There hasn't been a civilized nation in history that was able to avoid it, it's a definite must-do thing. This nation is in its infancy, and frankly without a monetary system it will stay there. To advance, even an inch, beyond where it is now, it must have currency that can be traded between individuals, businesses, the government, and other nations. It cannot be otherwise."

"Having said that, this currency has to based on something redeemable. Like a gold standard, but not a gold standard in this case because there's too much gold laying around now. In the recent past, the national currency was moved away from being based on anything redeemable. They could do this because they had started out with a redeemable currency and the citizens had built up a faith in it. I think it was a mistake to leave the gold standard, and trying to float a currency without a base standard now wouldn't work anyway."

"All right," said Adrian. "I'm with you so far."

Jeff continued. "My thought is to base the new currency on fuel, redeemable at the Corpus Christi refinery. One Texas dollar for one gallon of gasoline or diesel. To do this the republic has to take ownership of the oil coming into Corpus and of the refinery. In order to spread this currency and get the citizens to believe in it and to find it useful...I have a plan in mind. It's simple really. The new government establishes gas stations across its territory. To establish these gas stations, where the new currency can purchase fuel, the government sends out crews to pre-selected existing stations to put them back in working order, then supplied with tankers of fuel. Electricity to run each station will come from generators that are run off of a portion of the fuel that is regularly delivered. Each station will also be allocated currency to be distributed free to the area's citizens, each citizen being granted one hundred Texas dollars on a one-time basis. As these new Texas dollars spread, each individual will be able to engage in commerce with other individuals using the currency, slowly but surely replacing the current barter system. The official currency will be the only item that will be recognized for purchasing fuel from the station. It's a kick start, a boot strap operation. The fuel stations will be replenished with fuel as needed, but the currency will not be distributed again freely."

"The amount of currency placed into circulation will be calculated against the amount of fuel that can be produced in Corpus in one year. As production improves, more currency will be floated in a balanced amount. Eventually the amount of currency in circulation will be rationed such that it never exceeds more than fifty percent of the amount of fuel that can be produced in a given time...that's something we can't predict exactly right now though."

"At this point I'm guessing you're wondering just how this new government can make this happen. There's a plan, but I'll let the Admiral explain that part."

The Admiral began by saying "Before I do my part Adrian, do you have any questions for Jeff on what he's said so far?"

"No, he's explained it well enough, please go on; this is interesting."

"Well then let me go back a ways in time to give you some background. When the fleet dispersed to the various places around the nation our fervent hope was that the US government would re-establish itself and we would once again be under a civilian government. Militaries that aren't so constrained become very dangerous over time. But, and this is a big but, that hasn't happened; and we, the fleet commanders, have come to the conclusion that it won't happen. The survivors of the grid's dropping have no inclination to allow that government to come back. In a few places people have gathered together to try, but have failed each time. No one wants it back. Nearly no one that is. And the few that do are not trusted by the many that don't."

"We've discussed almost endlessly what to do, and have arrived at the conclusion that we will place the former United States Navy under the command of the Republic of Texas. It is the first credible and freely elected government to form since the disaster."

Adrian started to speak, but the Admiral raised his hand to stop him. "Whoa now, let me finish. We also speak for the other military branches, Army, Air Force, Marines of course, and Coast Guard. I hate to say it this bluntly, but like it or not you are now the Commander in Chief of the former United States Military. That's a lot to say and a lot to swallow, but hear me out, there's logic behind this. Believe me it's irrefutable, because we have all taken turns playing devil's advocate and the result, no matter how it's argued, came out the same way."

"Now, how does this tie into the currency question? It's simple, the Republic of Texas now owns the military and it's the military that is pumping and refining oil. By virtue of possession, the oil and its products belongs to the Republic, therefore the Republic can issue currency backed by the oil and its products. We have a great source of technology and knowledgeable and skilled men and women in Corpus. We've already set up a mint to stamp money. We've settled on aluminum coins for now, paper printing can come later. Counterfeiting is a problem for the future, the currency can be redesigned as the ability comes along."

"We've also thought through what to do with the military that is now at your disposal and our suggestion, and it's only a suggestion since you are now the CIC, is to leave the military where it is for now. We can begin refining oil in many places using nuclear powered ships at refineries, these can then distribute the Texas dollars and oil to various portions of the remaining continent and Hawaii and begin bringing order out of the chaos in those places."

"At some point in the future, this will probably lead to other sections of the country that will want to join the Republic of Texas, and while this may seem far-fetched right now, we believe it will happen. This is a government that has already proven itself even though it is in such an early stage. People want that, they want what you have wrought from the raw material of Texans, they want a stable currency... barter can only take you so far...they want law and order and the model is right here, right now, and nowhere else. In time I believe the entire former United States of America will become something akin to a Union of States of the Republic of Texas."

"A seed was planted in Cotulla when you were elected President and a new government was formed. This new government, based on individual sovereignty became a catalyst, and the social structure you have created will spread very fast. And some day the former U.S. Armed Forces will be back in the hands it belongs in, the people of this country. It'll be a different name, it'll be a different government, but it won't be a different people."

Adrian held his hand up stop the Admiral. "So let me get this straight. You're telling me that the entire United States Armed Forces, all branches of it, have decided that the federal government is dead and buried and the Republic of Texas is the first new government to self-create and that the military is handing over the keys to the Republic of Texas? Does that about sum it up?"

CHAPTER 29

"Yes Adrian, that pretty well sums it up. So what do you think so far?"

"I think it's too much to comment on without time to think it through. The currency idea appeals to me, but I want to think it over and consult with Congress on this. Our first full Congressional meeting starts in one week. I'll present it to them, and if you'll allow me to borrow Jeff to answer their questions, we'll put it to a vote. If it passes Congress my inclination right now is to sign the bill...but I also want to talk to Perry first and get his thoughts."

"Secondly, to the turning over of the military, I have an immediate reaction, and that is...no. There is no way on God's green earth that I want to assume command of it. Frankly I don't even know what Texas would do with it."

The Admiral replied. "I'm extremely glad to hear that. My biggest fear was that you would jump on it with both feet. It scares me no end to think of all that power aggregated into the hands of one man, or at least one man that actually wants that power. The fact that you don't want it is hugely reassuring and I'll sleep much better at night knowing you resisted ownership. However, I'm afraid that it's a done deal."

Adrian's face turned red and his hands clenched into fists. The Admiral was opening his briefcase as Adrian began to speak. "Damn it Admiral! It is not a done deal. I do not and will not accept."

The Admiral slid a two inch thick file across the table to Adrian. "Mr. President, and I say that knowing we are in your home, you have no choice in this matter. This folder contains the signatures of the Commandants of each of the branches of service. The signatures are appended to a document that turns full and total control over to the current sitting President of Texas and his successors. You simply have no choice in the matter. You have a heavy duty being imposed on you, and what you do with that duty is up to you. You can ignore us, or you can use us...we can't control that. What we can control we have done so by virtue of this document."

"Admiral do you realize that you are handing the greatest military in the history of the world into the hands of a simple ground-pounder? You're placing nuclear warheads and missiles at my command? You're telling me that I am supposed to be the supreme commander of the entire arsenal and the entire roster of this huge military machine? Do you even begin to comprehend how unqualified I am for that position? You've gone insane. Pure and simple."

Linda watched as Adrian dug into his position and knew that clenched jaw meant business. She also watched the Admiral who was relaxed and cool. It was obvious to her that the Admiral not only expected Adrian's resistance but as he had said, appreciated it. Watching the Admiral closely, she realized he would only be that relaxed facing

Adrian's refusal if he knew that the outcome was already ordained and Adrian's resistance couldn't stop the turnover from happening.

"Adrian...I'm sorry. This is a huge burden to place on any one man's shoulders. We've carried this burden jointly and it has truly been a burden on us. You must know that we will support you to our fullest abilities in any way we can. We will provide suggestions and information to you at every step of every decision if you so desire. But the plain fact is this, you are now the Commander in Chief, involuntarily as it may be. You've been drafted son, and there's no escaping it other than resigning as President...in which case the burden falls on your successor. You say you're not qualified, but if you'll remember the qualifications of past President's you'll realize that you are indeed far better qualified than the majority of them were. If it helps any, remember that your Constitution gives the power of declaring war only to Congress. Your main job will be to deploy military resources in a defensive posture and to oversee the day to day normal course of actions. If Congress declares a war then you'll have the advantage of the best military minds in existence to help you formulate strategy. It's not all bad, Adrian, not if you're clear-headed and willing to listen before making decisions."

"Look," the Admiral continued. "This has been pretty intense, too much to swallow on a moment's notice, I'm sure. Why don't we take a break and let's go see the girls. As frustrating as they are, I've grown genuinely attached to them and would like to see how they're doing. We can pick this up again tonight after you've had a little time to absorb it all."

Before Adrian could respond, Linda said, "That's an excellent idea. Come on gentlemen I'll lead the way. Adrian do you want to come or would you rather stay here and think a while?"

Adrian looked at Linda with an almost blank expression. "Hon, if you don't mind I think I'll stay here. Would you ask Roman, Matt, Perry, and Tim to come over? I need their advice on this."

"Sure thing, I'll do that on the way to the girl's dorm. We'll be back in a few hours."

Linda stopped in front of a large rambling house. "This is the girl's dorm." She stepped onto the porch and knocked on the door. Race opened it a moment later.

Linda said, "Brought you some visitors!" Then stood aside so that Race could see the Admiral.

"Admiral!" Race shouted and rushed to give him a bear hug.

The Admiral, not having left the girls on the best of terms, was surprised at the warm welcome. He had been expecting them to be stand-offish at best, and quite possibly hostile.

"Race, it's so good to see you. I've missed you girls more than you know. Life on ship has been dull since you left. Everyone misses you girls and sends their regards. They've commissioned me to ask you all to come for a visit soon...we'll provide a helicopter to take you back and forth."

"Awesome! When can we go? Linda, when can we go?"

Linda looked at the Admiral and raised one eyebrow.

The Admiral replied, "As soon as I clear it with Linda and Adrian. Maybe even starting tomorrow when I go back. It'll take a few trips to get all of you there. You girls can stay as long as Linda says. I don't want to interfere with your schooling, though. Speaking of schooling, why don't you show us around. You know Jose, this other gentleman is Lieutenant Parsons. I believe he'll be staying behind for a month or two."

Race took them on a tour of the house. After they settled down after the tour in the large room that doubled as a classroom and living room, she said, "See Admiral, we have everything in the world right here. We spend most of our time on military training which is great...but I know it's good for us to have regular schooling too so we stick it out on that. Discipline means doing things that need to be done even though you don't want to do it, as Adrian reminds us nearly every day." She said this last with a smile.

"I see you've added a new member?"

"Yes sir," Race said with pride. "Adrian's Angels are now the Women's Military Academy and Orphanage. The word is going out that orphans are welcomed at Fort Brazos. It was Adrian's idea, he wanted a safe place for kids without family. He said that military school training for orphans was just the ticket. The plan is to have a boy's academy and a girl's academy made up of Texas orphans. Eventually, when enough of us have reached the age of eighteen and graduated from the training we'll be formed up into the new Texas Rangers. Our mission will be much the same as the old Texas Rangers:

patrol the border and enforce the laws. The boys and girls, well men and women at that point, will be assigned to Ranger Companies that are assigned to specific patrol regions. We'll go from orphans to Rangers with an extremely important job to do for the Republic. We're all excited and can't believe how lucky we are. When I first saw Adrian, I knew things were going to change, but not this much. It's beyond my wildest dreams!"

"Why, I had no idea!" The Admiral said, "It's a splendid plan. Simply genius. That Adrian is one smart man, brilliant really...although he doesn't seem confident of his own abilities outside of knowing how to fight. This just reinforces everything I've thought of him. Outstanding."

"That reminds me Admiral." Linda interjected. "I've been wanting to ask you if we could borrow Ryan to teach a class in military history. It's just what the girls need the most right now. Any chance?"

"Absolutely. If you consent to letting the girls visit the ship, I'll send Ryan back with them and start right away. Linda I can't tell you what a morale lift it would be for everyone in Corpus to see the girls again. They really do miss them."

"It's a deal." Linda said with a smile. Race and the girls jumped up and whooped loudly.

That evening the Admiral and his men met with Adrian and his Kitchen Cabinet; Linda, Roman, Sarah, Matt, Perry, and Tim. Adrian said, "We've talked this over and have come to the conclusion that our only legitimate course of action is to present your offer of the military to Congress and let them decide. We've also come to the conclusion that Congress will accept."

"Just so." the Admiral replied. "It's exactly what we expected you would do, and once again I am happy to say it's what I wanted you to do. It proves to me again that I am right, that you are the right man for this. Any other process would have been...scary."

The Admiral opened his brief case for the second time and removed another thick folder of documents. "This is an operational readiness report. It contains information that we prefer be kept secret, for your eyes, and the eyes of your staff only and should be kept under lock and key. Every military installation, weapons inventory, number of men, the total count of equipment, and so on is in here. You'll want to study this carefully so that you know exactly what you have at your disposal. You'll also note that the location and disposition of nuclear weapons is included. We've gone to great lengths to keep the nuclear weapons secure...but they're in too many locations; we'd like you to consider consolidating several of them to reduce the number of areas we have to maintain. You'll find our proposed consolidation plan in the folder."

"And now that you've constructively accepted the post of Commander in Chief, I have to brief you on what we consider to be an imminent threat to the Republic of Texas and the rest of the country. China had been building ships at a feverish rate before the grid collapsed. They weren't nearly as damaged as we were by the CME. They were hit the same way we were, but while China had an emerging industrial complex to rival our own they were still a largely a non-electrified agrarian society. The farmers slightly out-numbered the urbanites. China was able to send most of its city folks out to live on the farms, which relied on human and animal labor, not electricity or tractors."

"The farmers absorbed the city people, putting them to work alongside them, which kept starvation to a bare minimum. The government then began slowly bringing back the engineers and scientists and then the skilled workers and were able to start up their infrastructure again. They are far ahead of us in that. But China needs energy, specifically they need coal and oil. The quickest way for them to get significant amounts of oil are from offshore drilling rigs, rigs that are already in place and just need to be started up again. They have begun sending their Navy out to take over all the rigs within their reach. Not only their navy but they've taken nearly all the ships from their neighbor countries too."

"Problem is, there aren't enough local rigs to supply their growing demand. They've begun reaching out further. Our intel suggests that they'll be heading for American waters soon. There are rigs all up and down our coasts, undefended rigs they can simply take by just pulling a ship up to them. Once they've taken those, it will be only a matter of time before they send massive amounts of ground troops onto our shores to take refineries and then into the interior to the major oil fields and coal mines. And by the way, Corpus Christi is a very rich target for them."

"I hate to lay this in your lap Mr. President, but it looks like you may someday be in a war with China."

CPSIA information can be obtained at www.ICGtesting.com
Printed in the USA
LVOW08s1550290616

494600LV00001B/52/P